Art, Vendors and Forgery
Apple Creek R-Park Department Mysteries
Book 2

Montie Red

RED

This book is a work of fiction. Names, characters, places and incidents are either product of the author's imagination or are used fictitiously. Any similarity to actual people (living or dead), events, or locales is entirely coincidental.

Copyright © 2025 Montie Red

All rights Reserved. No part of this book may be reproduced, scanned, distributed, or used in any printed, electronic, digital or any other form without the express permission of the author. Please do not participated in or encourage piracy.

ISBN: 978-1-962293-06-8

Editing by First Editing

Cover design: MRed

Map Illustrator: M Red

Library of Congress

 Created with Vellum

To my biggest and most interesting mystery in life, Josephine

Apple

City Hall

Bakery

Cyder's Pub

Creek

History
Art Museum

Ice Cream&Flower Shop

Chapter 1

I sighed as the pile of papers—just half an hour ago neatly reduced—grew higher once again. Linda kept adding more: summer activity registrations, the second session of summer camps, the farmer's market, and, of course, the Arts Festival.

"Most of these should be done by the end of the week," Linda said, her tone mirroring the defeat in my mind. "Then we can talk about the new budget presentation, the annual department report, and the assessment for the Council."

I let myself fall back into my chair, trying not to think about how many extra hours this would cost us.

"What we really need is for Martin to hire a

new Recreational Programs Director," I said. "When is he coming back?"

Linda threw her arms in the air, shaking her head. "Who knows? The state conferences ended last Tuesday. It's Thursday, and he still hasn't shown his little b—back in his office! Believe me, Margaret, if you think we're behind, the management department is living a nightmare."

I rested my chin on my hands and grabbed the top file from the pile. It was only 11 a.m., and I already felt exhausted. I understood Martin's hesitation. Over the past few weeks, I had grown closer to the people here, and in trying to get a grasp on the work, Martin, Linda, and I had spent plenty of lunches in his office. That's when we learned he was planning to propose to Tara.

Well... that wasn't going to happen anymore.

The last we heard, Tara, Rufus, and Mrs. Taylor were all in prison, waiting for the justice system to do its job. I didn't like thinking about it—I would have to testify in court, and I wasn't looking forward to it. I could only imagine how much worse it was for Martin, who would have to testify against Tara.

That said, his hesitation to fill her position

Art, Vendors and Forgery

was starting to wear on me. The department was already short-staffed, and although I did my best to share the burden, we were all reaching the end of our rope.

"I'm so glad you're here!" The Mayor's voice carried into the room from somewhere behind the mountain of paperwork.

Linda jumped at the same time I stood, sending half of the folders tumbling to the floor.

"Oh no!" he said, crouching down to help pick up the scattered papers. "I'm so sorry—I didn't mean to startle you."

I shot a glance at Linda, who was on the ground, clearly hiding her frustration. For the Mayor's safety, I decided we should have this conversation elsewhere.

"It's alright, Mayor," I said, taking his arm and steering him toward the door. "Linda, don't worry about these—I'll pick them up in a minute."

Linda rolled her eyes but continued stacking the papers, making me smile. I kept forgetting about her obsession with organizing and cleaning. Given the current state of the department, I was sure it was driving her insane.

Once we were in the hallway, I turned to him. "What can I do for you?"

"Well..." He exhaled, and I noticed his hesitation as he chose his words. "I know you're extremely busy, but I need your help with the festival."

I frowned, slowing my pace. "Mr. Mayor, I know it looks chaotic, but I guarantee the festival is on track. We have the vendors set up, the food trucks lined up, and we're coordinating with the schools to see which ones want to participate in the live events."

He nodded, but it wasn't reassuring. "I'm sure you're working on it, but I have someone who's been... very insistent about adding new elements to the festival."

"Mrs. Roberts?" I asked, biting my tongue to stop myself from saying what I really thought. Unfortunately, my silence must have come across as agreement.

"We have a meeting with her—right now," he announced. "She was on her way to my office when I ran to get you." He chuckled, which was both funny and mildly terrifying.

Although our working relationship had improved after last month's... events, we weren't exactly friends. He still pushed all my buttons during council meetings, and I was certain he hated my assertive responses—what my mom called *sassy remarks*.

"She's probably already in my office," he added. "So let's hurry, shall we?"

The Mayor's office was on the second floor of City Hall, making the walk from my office on the fourth floor short—sometimes, like that morning, *too* short.

As soon as the elevator doors opened, I spotted Chief Daniel Anderson waiting for us.

My heart leapt into my throat, my mind racing to fill the gap with the worst possible scenarios. After all, this wouldn't be the first time I'd walked straight into a crime investigation. The thought made me both anxious and, oddly, a little proud.

"Chief Anderson," Mayor Dosal said, coming to an abrupt stop. "Is everything all right?"

I didn't know Chief Anderson very well. I'd seen him at the police station a few times when I dropped off Bruno in the mornings, and Logan had introduced us before one of the council meetings. Our conversations had been limited to park safety and small talk. But if I had to define him in a few words, I'd say he loved his job, was polite, and was easy to talk to.

That morning, though, he looked nothing like his usual self. His shirt was buttoned unevenly, his hair was a mess, and he couldn't stop shifting his hands from his hips to his sides and back again. His expression wasn't reassuring, either, which immediately put both the Mayor and me on edge.

"I have—something happened and I—" He sighed, staring into the distance. "Yes, Apple Creek is fine. This is... personal."

"I'll wait for you in the office," I said, ready to walk away, but to my surprise, Chief Anderson gently grabbed my arm.

"No, please stay. You'll hear about this anyway."

Mayor Dosal's features softened, a flicker of compassion in his eyes.

"Is it your wife? We can talk in my office, Daniel."

"It's better here. I'm in a hurry." The chief took a deep breath before speaking again. "She had a heart attack last night. We rushed her to the hospital. She's stable now, but very delicate. I can't—I'm sorry, Henry, but I need to leave to be with her."

"There's nothing to be sorry about," the

Mayor said, and though I could already imagine the chaos of being without a police chief, his voice was sincere. "Take as much time as you need. Rachel is strong—she'll get through this."

Chief Anderson nodded, but he didn't look convinced.

"I'll give you a list of substitutes later—"

The Mayor shook his head. "Just go. Forget about this. We'll figure it out. Right, Margaret?"

I nodded, though I had no idea what *figuring it out* meant.

"I hope your wife gets well soon," I said as the elevator doors opened again. He gave me a small, grateful smile before stepping inside.

The Mayor said nothing until the elevator doors closed. Then, he let out a loud groan, running a hand through his hair.

"This is a disaster, Margaret!" He exhaled sharply. "Martin's out, now we don't have a chief. The council is going to eat me alive and —well, we still have the festival and—"

As if on cue, the next elevator opened, revealing Mrs. Roberts.

Her face lit up with a wide smile that matched her round cheeks, and she wore an elegant yet complicated outfit that looked more suited for an art gala than a morning meeting. In her hands, she barely managed to hold a bundle of paper rolls and brochures. She wasn't alone.

Beside her stood a tall, thin man in an expensive suit, his sharp gaze sweeping over the Mayor and me with quiet scrutiny.

"I'm so glad you could see me this early, Henry," Mrs. Roberts said in a sweet yet urgent tone. "I managed to convince our lovely museum director, Tristan DeVoir, to join us. This will be the best Arts Festival Apple Creek has ever seen."

Chapter 2

In a few minutes, the Mayor's desk overflowed with rolls of blueprints and large, color-coordinated schedules—a system Linda would appreciate. Across from him, the museum director looked as if he'd rather be undergoing a root canal, and the Mayor himself didn't seem far from that sentiment. He sat with his arms crossed, one hand rubbing his chin, as Mrs. Roberts enthusiastically explained her plans.

"I understand if you're concerned about the cost, Henry," Mrs. Roberts said in a sweet tone, her fingers grazing the papers as if they were made of glass.

"It's not just the cost, Mrs. Roberts—"

"Please, Henry, it's Catherine," she interrupted with a chuckle, flashing me a bright smile. "I don't believe in formality among coworkers. It only creates obstacles to better relationships." She leaned slightly toward me, lowering her voice, though the Mayor could still hear. "We both know the best way to get things done is by connecting with the people who do the work. That's the secret to success. Human connections are the ultimate goal in life."

I couldn't help but smile, even if I wasn't entirely sure I agreed with her philosophy. Across from us, the Mayor wasn't as amused but played along.

"In that case, Catherine, it isn't just about the money."

Mrs. Roberts placed a hand over her chest and leaned back, feigning offense. "You don't like my ideas?"

"No, no, Catherine! I like the—" The Mayor shook his head, trying to backtrack, but she didn't let him.

"So it's change you don't like? You always say we should embrace change, Henry, and now that you have the chance—"

"I think change is good, but the festival has been—"

"A disaster for the last decade! Henry, you know this."

Art, Vendors and Forgery

"The festival has been a perfect small-town tradition," the museum director cut in, raising his voice. "As it should be. Apple Creek, although charming, is still a small town."

"This small town, Tristan, has paid your exorbitant salary for years," Mrs. Roberts shot back, matching his tone. "It's time your little museum participates with the rest of the town. You are not the Met."

The Mayor turned to me, his desperation and frustration plain on his face. Sensing the growing tension, I decided to step in.

"Mrs. Roberts, as you know—"

"It's Catherine to you, too, hon," she corrected with a wink.

Once again, I found myself mirroring her smile, despite the anxiety she had when addressing the Mayor and the irritation she directed at the museum director.

"Thanks, Catherine. I'm not sure if you know, but I grew up in Apple Creek—"

She chuckled and settled into her chair. "Oh, I know, Margaret. I don't run in the same circles as your mother, but Mrs. O'Leary always talks to Mrs. Williams, who's an old friend of mine. I know all about you heading to the city for college, starting a family, and... well, we're happy you're back home."

Montie Red

I wasn't thrilled that my life was a topic of discussion around town, but I couldn't say I was surprised. That was just how Apple Creek operated.

"I'm glad to be back. But if you don't mind me asking, what exactly don't you like about the past festivals?"

Catherine sat up straight, gripping the armrests. "Did you miss the last ten years of them?"

For a second, her accusation stung. Then I reminded myself that my focus should be on improving the festival, not justifying my past visits.

"I don't remember the last one I attended—"

"Exactly my point!" Catherine turned back to the Mayor. "This is why we need to revamp this fiasco, Henry! The Art Festival should be a reason for tourists to visit and return every year —not just an event to entertain the neighbors."

The Mayor's eyes widened as he shook his head. "With all due respect, Catherine, my priority is the happiness of our residents. I won't use taxpayer money to turn Apple Creek into something it isn't."

The director's posture straightened, and for the first time, he looked satisfied. I wasn't entirely on Catherine's side, but I didn't like

Art, Vendors and Forgery

the self-satisfied smirk on Mr. DeVoir's face either.

"But we are a big city, Henry!" Catherine countered, her voice rising. For the first time, I saw the woman Martin had warned me about. "Apple Creek deserves leaders who believe in its full potential. The festival is a chance to showcase our uniqueness and talent. If you don't see that... I'm starting to understand what Fred meant when he warned me about your ways, Henry."

If I had thought the Mayor was angry before, I was mistaken. His face flushed red, his hands shook, and if a weapon had been within reach, Catherine Roberts might have met an untimely end.

"Councilman Roberts has irrational ideas for this town, Catherine. I can see now where he gets them."

At this rate, one of them might actually strangle the other, so I stepped in again.

"If the festival has been lacking impact, Catherine, I'd be happy to help improve it." Her smile was triumphant, but I wasn't finished. I turned to the Mayor. "And, of course, we must prioritize the well-being and interests of our residents."

Now, both of them turned their frustration on me. I had expected that.

"I believe we all want what's best for Apple Creek. The festival falls under the R-Parks Department, and I'm happy to work on Catherine's proposal within reasonable limits on spending, time, and resources."

After another three hours of debate, we reached a compromise. The Mayor agreed to add a culinary section, a candlelight fancy dinner-concert, and, pending approval from a curator and the city lawyer, a fine arts exhibit. The latter made the director visibly ill with concern, and frankly, I shared his unease. Mrs. Roberts, however, remained adamant about featuring an outdoor exhibit from the local history museum, including Apple Creek's most valuable painting by Sebastian Rodriguez.

"Just remember, Catherine," the Mayor cautioned as she prepared to leave. "If you want the piece displayed outdoors, you need the curator's approval. We have to ensure the sun won't damage it."

"Of course, Henry! I would never put the piece at risk," she assured him.

"And the city lawyer's approval. I won't increase our liability insurance over this."

Catherine's wide smile made it clear she

Art, Vendors and Forgery

had no concerns about the conditions. That only worried me more.

"Absolutely, Henry. I wouldn't have it any other way." She turned to me. "Margaret, I'll see you tomorrow at the museum at 10 a.m. And Tristan, don't be late. I know how much you enjoy rolling in after hours."

By the time I made it back to my office, the pile of folders seemed to have grown, and Linda's anxiety was at its peak. I wasn't looking forward to explaining to everyone the extra burden the festival would bring, but I had no choice. I called a department meeting.

Terry, Bert, Linda, and I made up the entire department, and it was clear we needed at least two more people—something I was going to demand from Martin. Immediately. Or at least as soon as I finished this meeting.

"Margaret, is the city shutting down the department?" Terry asked the second he walked into the room.

"Don't be absurd!" Bert exclaimed but shot me a quick look before adding, with more confidence, "This is about us getting more work."

Linda practically jumped out of her chair, shaking her head. "Margaret, no! We can't add more! We're already stretched so thin we're about to stop sleeping. It's impossible to take on anything else without—"

"Everyone, just take a deep breath," I said. Of course, no one calmed down. If anything, they looked even more concerned, and the tension in the room felt like a bouncing cap from a press cooker. I carefully chose my next words. "We definitely need more people in the department. After this, I'm going straight to Martin to demand he appoint them, even if it's just until the festival is over."

Linda's color started to return—until, of course, I continued.

"After meeting with the Mayor, Director DeVoir, and Mrs. Roberts, there will be a few changes to the festival."

That did it.

Bert threw up his arms, and Terry buried his face in his hands. The room erupted into a chaotic mix of complaints, but Linda's voice cut through the noise.

"Not again!"

"What do you mean, again?" I asked.

Bert let out a sarcastic chuckle. "Every year, we have to redesign this ridiculous festival," he

Art, Vendors and Forgery

grumbled, dropping into a chair. "I've been asked to move it from Central Park to the River Bluffs Preserve, only to have it relocated to the gym in the Community Center, and then to the City Hall parking lot!"

"And every single one was a disaster!" Linda shouted. "Mrs. Roberts will never be satisfied because she has nothing else to do, and this is her personal project."

"We can't do this again, Margaret," Terry added, his shoulders slumping. His eyes reflected nothing but exhaustion and defeat.

I felt awful for not knowing all of this before my meeting. After hours of negotiation, I had agreed to some of the proposed changes, assuming adjustments were necessary. But now, I realized the festival's alleged past failures weren't due to disorganization, as Mrs. Roberts had claimed—they were because of her constant last-minute interference.

"I should have known about this," I admitted, trying to sound reassuring. "The changes I agreed to aren't drastic, and I think they'll help the festival. We're staying in Central Park, keeping the vendor arrangement, but working around the gazebo to make room for live art performances—like music and dance. We had to

17

cancel the kids' part because we're short-staffed."

Linda, Terry, and Bert remained unimpressed. I needed a better sell.

"This year, we're highlighting our local culinary scene with a bake-off contest for residents, plus food stands so we can sample everything. And we'll be the judges—so, free food."

That, at least, got a reaction.

Bert chuckled. "I'm always in for free food."

"See? That's the attitude," I said, pressing on. "And we'll organize a candlelight dinner—which, of course, we'll get to attend."

"A candlelight dinner?" Linda shook her head. "What if it rains, Margaret? That's a disaster waiting to happen. And when it does, Mrs. Roberts will throw one of her annual tantrums and promise—" she lifted her fingers in air quotes— "'to make next year's festival the best one Apple Creek has ever seen.'"

"I won't let that happen, Linda," I said firmly. "Now that I know what's been going on, I'll put a stop to it. She won't keep interfering with our work."

Their expressions shifted slightly—hopeful but wary. I meant what I said. I wasn't a fan of people micromanaging others while refusing to

Art, Vendors and Forgery

take responsibility. From my previous conversation with Mrs. Roberts, I never would have guessed she'd been involved in the festival planning at all. That had to change.

"I'm also going to talk to Martin and get more help."

Bert let out another chuckle. "Really? And when exactly are you going to—"

"Right now." I grabbed my things and strode out of the room.

I was ready for a long conversation with Martin. Also, I wasn't eager to sit in my office. Too many files on my desk for my liking.

Chapter 3

Poor Martin. He really hadn't expected me to be so bossy and upset, but it all worked out. He agreed to loan us one of the IT assistants, Sophie Parker, and Norman Beltran, the Operation and Maintenance manager, until the festival was over, while he reviewed applications to fill Rufus and Tara's positions. I wasn't entirely sure that last part would happen, but I had a plan. I was going to force the mayor to push Martin into action. After all, he owed me now.

I was also going to have Norman put pressure on Martin—because I was certain poor Norman wouldn't be thrilled about being assigned to my department again.

"There you are!" My mom's voice rang through the office the second I walked in.

Art, Vendors and Forgery

"Mommy!" Darcy squealed, running straight into my arms.

Although I was thrilled to see them both, my mom's expression put me on edge.

"What happened?" I asked, hugging Darcy while trying to keep my tone light for her sake.

Darcy pulled back with a big smile, placing her small hands on my cheeks to make me look directly at her. "Grandma saw a guy."

"Darcy!" my mom hissed, glancing around.

I knew Linda heard, even though she was at her desk pretending to be busy.

"I told you to wait until we got to her office," my mom scolded.

Darcy just giggled and grabbed my hand, leading me toward my office. By now, she knew the way very well. Though I had no intention of staying there longer than necessary, my sweet Darcy loved visiting, especially when she got to take over my desk and pretend she was in charge. Some days, I wondered if she would do a better job than me—even at just five years old.

My mom stepped inside and closed the door. Not satisfied, she went to the window and shut the blinds, something I had never done before.

"Mom?"

She rubbed her face and paced the room. "It was awful, Margaret. Why would he—? I mean, we haven't talked since... Christmas? A little warning would have been nice. He was supposed to be somewhere in Europe, not in Apple Creek."

Darcy, still giggling, rested her hands on the desk as she watched my mom have a meltdown.

"Who, Mom?"

"Benjamin!"

"Benjamin? Who is—" My stomach churned as I remembered the smiling face of my mother's former long-term boyfriend, our old police chief. "You mean Ben? Ben Morales?"

My mom sighed dramatically. "Yes, Margaret! Who else?"

She finally stopped pacing and leaned against the door. But it was Darcy who actually explained what had happened.

"We were supposed to have lunch, Mommy," she said, wearing an all-knowing expression beyond her years. "But when we got out of the car outside the Cyber Bar, Grandma just froze."

"The Cyber Bar?" I repeated, confused.

Darcy rolled her eyes. "Grandma's favorite soup place, Mommy! But that's not the point."

Art, Vendors and Forgery

"You mean Cyder's Pub?"

Darcy threw up her hands. "What is a pub if not a bar, Mommy?"

I pressed my lips together, stifling a laugh—and mild irritation at how much she sometimes sounded like her father.

"All right, so Grandma froze. Then what?"

"I didn't freeze," my mom corrected. But then, a burst of laughter escaped her, and between the giggles, I pieced together the rest: she had shoved Darcy back into the car, jumped into the driver's seat, and sped all the way here.

I laughed too, until my mom sobered and asked the question that sent dread pooling in my stomach.

"Why would he come back, Maggie?"

I wished the blinds were open so I could signal Linda—or anyone—to come rescue me. My mom, now staring at me with narrowed eyes, was not someone to be trifled with.

"What do you know?" she demanded.

I hesitated. Chief Anderson's situation wasn't really my business to share... but I also wasn't about to keep secrets from my mother.

"I can't be sure, Mom, but I accidentally found out this morning that Chief Anderson is taking a leave of absence because of his wife's health."

My mom's expression shifted instantly. She placed a hand on her chest, all previous hysteria vanishing. "Oh no. I didn't know Martha was so sick. I thought she was doing better."

Then, the same realization I had earlier dawned on her. Her eyes widened. "Oh boy. You think Ben is here because of the position? As a substitute? Would he become chief again?"

I put up my hands. "I don't know, Mom. The mayor is looking for a temporary replacement, but I have no idea who it'll be." I hesitated. "Ben being here is... suspicious, though."

My mom sank into a chair and covered her face. "What am I supposed to do now? Should I call him? Ignore him? This is different than sending a birthday card or a short holiday call."

"I don't know, Mom. Maybe just... wave next time you see him?"

She frowned at me.

Darcy, of course, laughed even harder.

As soon as the elevator doors opened on the first level, Darcy marched straight toward the police station. It was so nice to see her smiling, walking with confidence in her new town. Over the past few weeks, I'd noticed a change in her. Though still shy, she had started talking more to the people she'd met.

Outside the station, Logan stood talking to an older man in uniform. His arms were crossed, his expression severe. The tension in the air made Darcy stop in her tracks. She turned to me and slipped her hand into mine. Their voices were muffled, but even from a distance, I could tell it wasn't a friendly conversation. The absence of a certain furry K-9 officer only added to my unease.

"I won't tolerate any shortcuts this time," the older man was saying when Logan noticed us. "Do you understand me?"

Logan's expression didn't change. Instead of answering, he turned toward us. "Deputy Warren, let me introduce you to the R-Parks director, Margaret Willow."

If I was caught off guard, the deputy was downright shocked to find Darcy and me standing just a few steps away.

"Deputy, it's nice to meet you," I said, extending my hand.

He shook it briefly, attempting a smile at Darcy, but whatever had been discussed before our arrival still lingered on his mind.

"Pleasure to meet you, Miss Willow. I'm sure we'll be working closely over the next few weeks." Then, turning back to Logan, he added, "I need that information by tomorrow morning, Forest."

Logan's jaw tightened. He said nothing.

The deputy seemed satisfied with the lack of response and, with one last glance at Darcy, walked past us. I watched him go, not daring to speak.

As soon as he was out of earshot, Logan exhaled sharply, then crouched down to Darcy's level.

"Now, what do I owe the pleasure of seeing you in this dump?"

Darcy giggled, her grip on my hand relaxing. "Grandma needed space."

Logan's eyebrows shot up. He glanced between us before settling his gaze on me. "What did your mom do this time?"

"Hey!" I protested, frowning at him, but Darcy answered before I could defend myself.

"Where's Bruno?"

Logan sighed dramatically. "Of course, you're here for him and not me. You're breaking my heart, Darcy."

My daughter shook her head, and sud-

Art, Vendors and Forgery

denly, I understood why my mom had wanted to run.

"My mom likes you more than Bruno."

Logan visibly froze. He opened his mouth as if to respond, then shut it, clearly struggling for words. When he finally looked at me, his expression was unreadable. Instead of addressing the comment, he redirected the conversation.

"Well, Darcy, your friend Bruno was just about done, but Tricia needed him. You remember her? The nice officer at the desk?"

Darcy nodded eagerly and turned to me, oblivious to the fact that my face was burning. "Let's go, Mommy! I can't wait to see him!"

I cleared my throat and was about to follow when Logan stopped me.

"Actually, Darcy," he said, his tone more serious now. "Why don't you go ahead and get him? Tricia's right there, and I need to talk to your mom about some boring work stuff."

Darcy looked up at me for approval—something that filled me with pride.

"Can I, Mommy?"

"Of course, Sunflower. Go on, I'll be right here."

She darted off, disappearing around the

corner. The moment she was gone, Logan's face darkened again.

"What is it?" I asked as we stepped slightly away from the hallway.

"You heard about Chief Anderson, right?"

I nodded.

Logan ran a hand through his hair, exhaling sharply. "So, the guy you just met—Deputy Warren? Let's just say we don't see things the same way."

I didn't disagree, but something about Logan's expression unsettled me. "May I ask—?"

"Let's just say we have history. One that's hard to forget."

A cold knot formed in my stomach. I hated seeing him like this—so guarded, so upset. And I hated that I didn't know him well enough yet to understand what he was going through.

"In any case, that's not why I wanted to warn you," he continued. "If the Mayor decides to give him Chief Anderson's position, the whole city is going to feel it. Warren believes in using power over connections. He'll crack down on policies, and your department won't be exempt. He could make your events a nightmare."

The tower of files on my desk flashed through my mind, along with Mrs. Roberts'

Art, Vendors and Forgery

plans for the art festival—where among other safety issues, she wanted to display an invaluable piece of art in the park for the weekend. A chill ran down my spine.

"That wouldn't be good," I murmured. "Do you think if I talk to the Mayor, he might—?"

Logan frowned, his expression stopping me mid-sentence.

"I think our Mayor avoids confrontation. And Deputy Warren excels at it."

I sighed, already picturing the uphill battle ahead. Maybe Mrs. Roberts would rethink her festival plans now—but I didn't have much hope.

"Mommy!"

Darcy's voice broke through my thoughts. She came bounding back with a huge grin, Bruno trotting at her heels.

I crouched to pet him, feeling an immediate sense of relief. Somehow, these two always made the day brighter—no matter how stressful it had been.

"You want to join us for lunch?" I asked Logan, thinking he could use a break.

He hesitated, then shook his head. "Ladies, I'd love nothing more than to join you, but I've got paperwork to finish. Late night, for sure."

Darcy surprised him with a sudden hug. He blinked, then smiled as he returned it.

"I'll save you some ice cream, Logan!" she promised.

Something softened in his gaze.

I smiled. "We'll have ice cream for you if you need some later—or tomorrow."

Logan smirked. "Now that's an offer I might take you up on."

Chapter 4

"That was a very nice offer from you, Darcy. I'm sure Logan will love his rainbow ice cream," I told my daughter as we walked through the park with our cones in hands and two pints in a bag, making our way toward our favorite bench by the pond.

"Thanks, Mommy!" she said, her face lighting up. "He needs to try more than just vanilla."

I chuckled at the thought of Logan attempting to eat a bright-colored, extremely sweet ice cream. Especially since Darcy was right—he was strictly a vanilla or chocolate person. That much hadn't changed since high school. At least now she knew not to mess with

Grandma's favorite—pistachio. Hence the second pint in the bag.

"Mom!" Darcy suddenly stopped in her tracks.

"What is it?" I asked, scanning the area for the usual culprits—an insect in her way or a particularly interesting bird perched on a tree.

"It's the man," she said, pointing toward a distant bench by the path. "The one Grandma was so concerned about. The mean guy."

My heart skipped a beat.

Sitting on the bench, his arms resting on his knees as he tossed crumbs to the birds, was Benjamin Morales—a man I had once considered my second father for seven years.

"Darcy, Ben is not a mean man." I searched for the right words to explain the complicated situation to my five-year-old. It was a conversation I had never imagined having, yet here we were. I could only guess she was feeling the same confusion I had felt years ago when my mother severed ties with him. Only I had been an adult then.

"Just like your dad, he had different plans than Grandma," I said carefully.

"Oh." Darcy's gaze lingered on Ben, studying him as if trying to solve a puzzle. "But

Art, Vendors and Forgery

he's back. Maybe Grandma should talk to him, right?"

That was a dangerous area for me. I didn't know how my mother felt now, but I knew that everything between Andrew and me was done. The last thing I wanted was to give Darcy false hope about reconciliation where none existed.

"How about you meet him first?" I suggested, squeezing her hand gently as we continued down the path. "Did you know he's the one who found Bruno in the first place?"

As if on cue, Bruno seemed to pick up Ben's scent. He perked up, tail wagging, and started tugging me forward with renewed excitement.

Darcy's eyes widened. "Really? He found Bruno?"

"He did," I confirmed. "Before Logan, before the station—Ben was the first person to take care of him."

Darcy's grip on my hand tightened as we got closer, her small face scrunching in thought. "Then maybe he's not that mean after all."

I glanced at Ben, who still hadn't noticed us. His profile was the same—strong, familiar

—but there was a weight to his shoulders now that hadn't been there before.

"Maybe not," I murmured, more to myself than to her.

And with that, we took the final steps toward the past I had long tried to leave behind.

Ben barely had a second to react before Bruno launched himself forward, planting two paws on his lap and pressing a wet nose against his face.

"You've grown!" Ben laughed, muffled somewhere behind a tangle of fur. "Although your behavior hasn't changed much."

I could have called Bruno off, but it was too much fun watching Ben genuinely laugh—something I hadn't seen him do in a long time. The last time I saw him, he was heartbroken and ready to leave town.

"Come on, Bruno." I gently pulled on his collar. After a moment of hesitation, Bruno reluctantly stepped back—just enough to sit directly on Ben's legs.

Ben chuckled as he looked up. "Maggie!"

Art, Vendors and Forgery

He stood, wrapping me in a warm, familiar hug. "It's so good to see you. How is—"

His gaze dropped to the little girl gripping my hand so tightly her knuckles were turning white. She peeked at him from behind my legs.

"Oh boy." Ben knelt with a bright smile. "You look just like your mom. You know, I met you when you were traveling in your mom's belly."

Darcy took a small step to the side, loosening her grip—just a little. Bruno, ever the troublemaker, shifted his weight, nudging Ben hard enough to make him lose balance and fall onto his backside.

"This guy," Ben said, scratching Bruno's ears. "Still causing trouble. Does he at least stop eating socks?"

"I'm not sure," I admitted. "Darcy's been losing socks since she was a baby, so for all I know, he still has a stash somewhere."

Ben grinned as he stood. "Are you accusing me of losing my own socks, Maggie?"

Darcy chuckled, taking another step away from me, and to my surprise, I felt an unexpected warmth in my chest. I hadn't realized how much I wanted her to like Ben, and as she settled on the bench beside him and we started chatting, it felt... like family.

35

I didn't dare ask why he was in town—not after what Logan had told me about the new chief's substitute. If Ben was just passing through, it wouldn't just be my mom's heart on the line this time.

"Margaret!" someone shouted down the path, "Thank goodness I found you!"

I had only met Mrs. Roberts once before, but I was sure I'd never forget her voice.

"It's an emergency!" She was slightly out of breath from rushing down the path. "Tristan DeVoir wants to send it away! We can't let this happen—it would be a massive loss for Apple Creek!"

Ben kept his attention on Bruno while Darcy swung her feet, but I noticed the way he stiffened slightly. The fact that my daughter seemed more intrigued by Mrs. Roberts than he did made his disinterest more suspicious.

"Come on! The museum is about to close," Mrs. Roberts urged.

"Catherine," I said as calmly as possible, "we have an appointment with him tomorrow. There's no need to—"

"That's the problem, Margaret!" She threw her hands up, her voice rising. "He's the one giving the piece away!"

Art, Vendors and Forgery

"The piece?" Ben finally spoke up, drawing Mrs. Roberts' attention.

"The Rodriguez!" she exhaled, flopping onto the bench dramatically. "That beautiful, remarkable, one-of-a-kind piece of art... and he wants to send it to Maple Hollow."

She turned to Darcy, patting her leg with sincerity. "Sweet child, you understand, don't you?"

Darcy glanced at me for a moment before solemnly nodding. "I wouldn't want anyone taking my Silly away."

"Your... Silly?" Mrs. Roberts repeated, her interest surprisingly genuine.

Darcy sighed dramatically. "My little angel figurine. Mommy gave it to me when I was born. It's unvaluable."

I chuckled. "You mean invaluable, sunflower."

Darcy dismissed my correction with a wave of her hand and turned back to Mrs. Roberts. "You understand, right?"

Mrs. Roberts gave her a side hug. "I do, sunflower. I do."

Ben and I couldn't help but laugh.

Mrs. Roberts suddenly squinted at Ben. "Do I know you? You look familiar."

Ben hesitated before replying, "I used to live around here. I'm just visiting a friend."

"Oh." She didn't seem convinced but, thankfully, didn't press the issue. Instead, she turned back to me. "So, what are we going to do? We can't let him give away our legacy. Don't you think?"

"I agree, but we can talk to him tomorrow. He's probably just loaning—"

Mrs. Roberts shot up so fast that even Bruno snapped to attention, ears back and tail stiff.

"It's a boycott, Margaret! Tristan is sending the painting tonight so we won't have access to it for the festival! We have to stop him!"

I really didn't want to ask how she knew all this.

For a second, Ben's timing seemed perfect —until he opened his mouth.

"I'm not sure how much you can do to stop the museum director," he said, then added, "but I can take Darcy home." His face brightened. "I still remember how to get there."

"Perfect!" Mrs. Roberts answered before I could. "Take this guy, too." She gestured at Bruno.

I was on the verge of telling Mrs. Roberts I

wasn't at her disposal when, Darcy jumped up, grabbed Bruno's leash, and hugged me.

"Bye, Mommy!" she said, her mischievous grin barely hidden.

Then she tried to wink—both eyes scrunching closed in an exaggerated frown. She leaned in and whispered, "Grandma will love this."

My heart sank as I watched her walk off with Ben and Bruno. I wasn't worried about her safety, but I was worried about my mom. And whatever funny ideas my little girl might be cooking up.

I could only hope those ideas didn't involve me and her dad later on.

"Come on, Margaret!" Mrs. Roberts urged. "I have a car waiting."

Chapter 5

The museum was one of the oldest mansions in Apple Creek, perched atop one of the surrounding hills. I had never thought of it as eerie, but arriving after hours, with the gates locked and the sun down, cast an unsettling shadow over the place.

"Tristan's office is by one of the patios," Catherine said as she strode past the garden gate, completely ignoring the sign that read *Staff Only*.

The proximity to the woods only heightened my nerves. Suddenly, I regretted not bringing Bruno or asking Ben to come with us. But ahead of me, Catherine moved with unwavering confidence—clearly, this wasn't her first time taking an unauthorized tour of the mansion.

Art, Vendors and Forgery

"How do you know Mr. DeVoir is sending the piece to Maple Hollow?" I asked, quickening my pace to keep up. "I know you mentioned an email, but did he send it to you directly?"

Catherine chuckled as she reached the patio's side door. "Of course not! He'd never tell *me* about his macabre plans. But," she paused for dramatic effect, "I *happen* to be a big anonymous donor to the Historical Preservation of the Valley. That means I get blind-copied on any information regarding the movement of historical pieces."

A new kind of respect—tinged with unease—settled in. Who knew how many ways she had to keep track of things that interested her? No wonder the mayor seemed to let her do as she pleased. And now, here I was, about to trespass in a closed museum to stop its director from making a business transaction.

If the mansion had looked ominous from the outside, the inside was downright unsettling. It wasn't abandoned—far from it, as the polished floors and pristine displays attested—but the dimly lit hallways, the shadowed corners of unlit rooms, and the faint echo of our footsteps were enough to put my nerves on alert.

"This way, hon," Catherine called over her shoulder. "Don't let the spirits of the past get to you."

A shiver ran through me, and before I could stop myself, I glanced behind me. A sudden, irrational sense of being watched gripped me.

"Oh, Margaret!" Catherine burst into laughter. "You poor thing! I didn't mean to scare you—I was just teasing."

I forced a smile, though part of me wanted to shove her for it, while the other part was still making sure *nothing* was actually following me. Meanwhile, Catherine strode forward, her heels clicking against the wooden floors. I took a deep breath, reminding myself there were no such things as ghosts.

Then, as we passed one of the exhibit rooms, something in the shadows shifted.

I paused, peering into the dim space. The lighting in the far end of the room flickered strangely, as if something—or someone—had moved.

Against all rational thought, I stepped inside. For a brief second, I was sure I saw movement near the back of the room. I was about to take another step when—

Art, Vendors and Forgery

A loud *crash* shattered the silence behind me.

I gasped and my pulse quickening as I bolted from the room and almost collided with Catherine, who'd stopped short in the hallway.

"Did you hear—" she started to say when a high-pitched scream cut through the mansion.

Without thinking, I pushed past her, following the sound. We rushed into a large, open room lined with shelves displaying art and historical artifacts. At first, nothing seemed out of place. Then, as I moved farther in, I saw it.

Near the far end of the room, bathed in the eerie glow of the moonlight filtering through a massive window, lay a man.

A woman knelt beside him.

"Oh my!" Catherine gasped, covering her mouth. But her wide eyes weren't fixed on the man—they were staring at the wall.

I ran toward the man, shouting over my shoulder. "Call 911! He needs help!"

Part of me expected to find Mr. DeVoir, but as I knelt beside the figure, I realized I didn't recognize him. His large frame was dressed in a crisp plaid suit and bow tie, his hair a mix of black and gray. A cane lay discarded nearby.

His eyes were closed. His chest—motionless.

"I found him like this," the woman murmured.

I turned toward her—and immediately recognized her.

Dana.

The same Dana who had worked at the tavern when Mr. Larry was murdered. The same Dana who had abandoned Logan when he was nearly wrongly accused of a crime.

The irony of the moment hit me like a punch to the gut.

"Margaret!" Catherine's voice snapped me out of my thoughts. Though she had her phone in hand, she wasn't speaking into it. Her eyes remained locked on the wall.

"The painting! It's—oh no!"

"We need an ambulance!" I shouted. "Catherine, *now!*"

I didn't know if the man still had a chance, but a life was more important than any stolen artwork.

Still, I followed her gaze to the empty space on the wall.

The Sebastian Rodriguez painting.

I had seen it several times before—its surreal blues and swirling sky had always drawn me in.

Now, it was gone.

A cold, blank expanse of white remained where the masterpiece had once hung.

"What in the—no!!" said the furious voice belonged to Tristan DeVoir, who had just entered the room.

He froze, taking in the scene—first the lifeless man, then the empty wall.

"We need the police!" he roared. "This is a robbery!"

As I sat on a bench in the museum's lobby, I couldn't help but wonder—how did I once again end up surrounded by police tape, uniformed officers, and a dead body in a room far too close for comfort?

I debated calling my mom to explain why I wasn't home, but I doubted that was a good idea. By now, she had likely met with Ben, and I had no idea how that had gone. Instead, I called Sandie, keeping it brief.

"Something came up at the museum," I told her, hoping she wouldn't press for details.

Before I could dwell on it further, Officer Tricia Green approached, a notebook in hand.

"Margaret," she said, her voice calm but professional. "Can I take your statement?"

I nodded and stood, following her toward an office on the mansion's main level. Relief washed over me that it was Tricia and not Deputy Warren conducting the interview. Maybe it was unfair, considering I had never even met the man, but Logan's warnings and the way Warren reminded me of Officer Collins —the corrupt cop who once tried to frame Logan and me—made trusting him impossible.

"Do you want to start by explaining why you were in the museum after hours?" Tricia asked, her tone almost apologetic.

"Of course." I took a seat across from her, but before she could do the same, raised voices echoed down the hallway.

Catherine.

"If you had anything to do with this," she snapped, her words sharp as a blade, "I swear, you'll regret the moment you took this job."

Tricia gave me a look that clearly said, *Stay here*, then moved toward the door. I had no choice but to listen.

"If you think you can come in here and threaten me in my own—"

Art, Vendors and Forgery

"Mr. DeVoir." Tricia's voice cut through the argument, sharp with authority. Gone was the apologetic tone she had used with me. "I suggest you remain in your office while we take statements."

"This woman was verbally assaulting me!" DeVoir protested. "I would assume the police are here to protect the innocent."

"And you'd be right," another voice interjected—deep, measured, and unfamiliar. The air grew tense.

"Mr. DeVoir," the man continued, his tone making it clear he wasn't interested in protests. "I have a few questions for you. Mrs. Roberts, go home and be sure to stay in town."

Catherine passed by the office door, chin held high, but something in her expression wasn't quite as confident as usual. I wanted to call out to her, to ask what had just happened, but Tricia reappeared in the doorway before I had the chance.

"Sorry about that," she said with a small sigh. "Shall we?"

I sat back down, but curiosity got the better of me. "Who was questioning Mr. DeVoir?"

Tricia hesitated before answering. "Deputy Warren." She exhaled and muttered, "I wish

Chief Anderson were here. He's much more understanding than—"

She abruptly cut herself off, eyes widening as she covered her mouth. A faint flush crept into her cheeks. "I shouldn't have said that. Please keep it between us?"

"Of course," I said, though her words only fueled my unease. "He makes me nervous."

Tricia gave a small nod, focusing on her notebook. "That makes two of us. Don't get me wrong, he's a good boss, but... his methods are very different from Chief Anderson's."

Tricia and I finished within a few minutes. I really didn't have much to say, and once I explained what I knew and saw, she seemed satisfied. As she walked me back to the lobby, she explained that she might reach out if she had any more questions.

I was on my way out when Deputy Warren emerged abruptly from an office on the far side of the lobby. If he wasn't happy before, now he was outright furious. I barely had time to step out of his way.

"What is he—?" He started shouting, then

Art, Vendors and Forgery

stopped abruptly when he saw me. He visibly reined himself in and addressed me in a slightly calmer tone. "I'm sorry, Miss Willow. Officer Green, did you finish taking her statement?"

Beside me, Tricia cleared her throat and forced her voice to sound steady. "Yes, sir. I was just telling her we'll reach out if we have any further questions."

Deputy Warren's gaze landed on me. "If you remember anything else—anything at all—contact Officer Green or me."

I opened my mouth to respond, but he was already striding across the lobby. "I'm not done with her," he barked at an officer halfway up the grand staircase.

The poor guy nodded before hurrying upstairs. As I followed his movement, two figures appeared on the second-floor open hallway. The first was Dana, and right behind her, I recognized Logan.

Deputy Warren took the stairs two at a time. "You can't be here, Officer Forest. You know this is a conflict of interest."

Dana and Logan stopped in their tracks. To my surprise, Logan didn't argue. He simply crossed his arms and waited for the deputy to reach them. The moment Warren did, their voices dropped into murmurs I couldn't make out.

A knot of concern tightened in my stomach as I turned to Tricia. "Please tell me I'm not the reason Logan can't work this case."

The second I said it, I regretted it. I shouldn't be a conflict. Logan and I were just friends. Maybe better friends than we'd been in years, but still—just friends. The admission left a sharp discomfort in my chest, one I found more annoying than I cared to admit.

Thank goodness, Tricia assumed I was talking about Bruno.

"Oh no," she assured me with a smile, holding the museum door open for me. "Your family fostering Bruno isn't a conflict. Besides, you're a witness, not a suspect."

I let out a relieved breath. At least I wasn't a problem—or under suspicion. But then, against my better judgment, I asked the question I didn't want answered.

"So why can't Logan—"

"Dana," Tricia said, shaking her head. "Even as an ex-wife, it could be a conflict. And honestly? I don't think Logan would be objective with her involved in this crime."

Chapter 6

As I walked into my house, my mind was a mess. On one hand, I had nothing to say to Logan. I knew he'd gotten married long ago and divorced a couple of years back. I could blame myself for never asking about his personal life, but I didn't feel like I had the right.

Which brought me to the other hand—anger. Why didn't I have the right to ask him?

"There you are!"

My mom's voice made me jump. She was sitting in the dark kitchen, nearly sending my heart into overdrive.

"Mom! Are you trying to give me a heart attack? What are you doing sitting in the dark?"

The bright kitchen light flicked on, momentarily blinding me. As my vision adjusted, I saw my mom standing there, arms crossed, looking far too serious.

I sighed, certain that someone had already filled her in about the museum incident.

"Mom, it's not like I wanted to be there when it happened."

"To be—Margaret! Do you know how it felt to open the door and, instead of finding my beautiful daughter, I found the man I *clearly* told you I just ran away from? With my Darcy? And *ice cream*?"

Ah. That minor detail had slipped my mind. But despite her effort to stay stern, I caught the undertone of happiness she was trying to suppress.

"And how did it go?"

Her whole demeanor shifted. She suddenly looked like a giddy sixteen-year-old, barely able to contain her excitement.

"I *froze* when I saw him. But then... oh, Maggie, I don't know."

She sat on a stool, resting her face in her hands. "I'm too old to feel this way."

"Mom!" I sat across from her, taking her hand. "There's no age limit on love."

"I'm not in—"

I held up a hand, stopping her mid-sentence. "You *are* in love. You never forgot Ben. Time just made it easier to live without him. Having Tobby and Darcy probably helped, but you still love him."

She pressed her lips together, sighing. "Was it that obvious?"

I patted her hand and leaned closer. "You *did* burst into my office."

She laughed, shaking her head, but her joy quickly turned into something more fragile.

"What if he doesn't—what if he's leaving? This time, it'll hurt even more, and I don't know if—"

I wrapped my arms around her. "Talk to him. One of the perks of being older than a teenager is that you can actually ask."

"Margaret!" she groaned against my shoulder, making me laugh. I pulled back and met her gaze.

"Just ask. He's a good guy. I don't think he'd ever hurt you on purpose."

Her eyes searched mine, filled with sadness and hope.

"No, Mom," I said, walking toward the fridge. "I'm *not* in love with Andrew, and he's not coming back." I raised a hand before she could argue, opening the fridge as the cold air seeped into the room, grounding me.

"Ben *asked* you to go with him. Andrew asked me to stay behind and raise our daughter alone. We were never part of his next chapter. And honestly? That didn't surprise me."

My mom nodded, her expression hardening. "If I ever see him again, he's *going* to hear what I have to say."

I smiled at that and turned back to my search for a late-night snack. Though talking to my mom had helped my mood, I still felt the undeniable craving for something sweet.

"Did you eat all the ice cream?"

"Wait a second," my mom said, her tone dripping with suspicion. "What did you mean earlier? *You didn't want to be there*? Darcy told me you were going to the museum with Catherine Roberts. What happened?"

I turned slowly, my appetite vanishing. How had I not seen this coming?

"There was a robbery at the museum," I mumbled, then rushed through the rest. "When Catherine and I arrived, someone had stolen the special piece. You know, the one by Sebastian Rodriguez? I think Sandie really liked it when we were in school."

"Oh my goodness!" My mom gasped, covering her mouth. "That's terrible!"

Art, Vendors and Forgery

"I know! It was a beautiful painting. Catherine was in shock."

She threw her arms up. "I *bet* she was! And I'm sure the director is just devastated. It was just on the news. Sebastian Rodriguez was admitted to a hospice upstate a month ago and died last week.

That caught my attention.

"I thought he was a *young* artist."

My mom laughed. "Well, of course he was! We were born the same year."

"Wow, that old?"

"Excuse me?"

I stumbled over my words, reaching for her as she huffed and walked out of the kitchen.

"Come on, Mom! Everyone at the museum called him a *young* artist. Darcy's a young artist! *I'm* an old artist."

My mom flopped onto the couch, shaking her head. "Darcy's a young artist? Really?"

"She is," I said, then quickly changed the subject. "No wonder they killed the curator. That painting is probably even more valuable now."

My mom's eyes widened. She leaned forward. "*What do you mean they murdered the curator?*"

I smacked a hand over my face, groaning at

my own loose tongue. How was I *this* bad at keeping things from her?

"I didn't want—"

"You *didn't want* to what? Worry me? Were you with the police? Please tell me at least Logan was with you."

At that, I groaned even louder and flopped onto the other couch. "Yes, I talked to the police. I gave my statement. And no, I'm not in any trouble." My gaze drifted to the coffee table between us as my voice growing quieter. "Logan was there, but not working. His ex-wife is a suspect."

"Oh no! I forgot she worked there. That must be hard on him."

For the first time since high school, I seriously considered *murdering* my mother.

"Well, I *guess* it is," I muttered, standing up and stomping toward the stairs. "Good night, Mom. I have *a lot* of work in the morning."

Chapter 7

I wasn't looking forward to dropping off Bruno that morning. The last thing I wanted was to talk to Logan. I was still mad at him, and it didn't even make sense. The last thing I needed was to sound jealous—because I wasn't. I just didn't like that it had to be Dana. We didn't have a great history, and I had never liked her. It almost felt personal, which made even less sense. Again, not jealous.

At the same time, a small part of me hoped he would explain himself when he saw me. After all, he had kind of ignored me last night, and that was a hard pill to swallow.

All too soon, I found myself crossing City Hall's lobby. Bruno had been walking calmly at my side—until that moment, when he suddenly decided it was time to rush ahead.

"Bruno!" I hissed, not wanting to draw attention to myself. The place was mostly empty at this hour, but still. "Stop, Bruno."

"Hey, buddy!" A familiar voice called out.

Ben.

Bruno didn't hesitate. He leaped up on his hind legs, showering Ben with an enthusiastic greeting. I didn't even bother stopping him this time—Ben could handle it.

"I'll get to you in a second, Maggie," Ben said, trying to push Bruno down.

I chuckled, but the moment of levity was cut short when the police station doors swung open, and three officers walked out.

"This isn't right!" Logan's voice rang through the hall, but at his side, Deputy Warren didn't slow down.

"Down," Warren commanded.

Bruno immediately obeyed, sitting with perfect posture, his tail stilling as he shifted into full K9 mode.

"Benjamin Morales?" Warren said.

I didn't need to hear the rest to know exactly what was happening.

Not that Logan was going to let me miss it—he stepped in front of his boss, voice rising.

"You don't have enough proof. Not to

Art, Vendors and Forgery

mention, this is completely disrespectful and—"

"Believe it or not, Forest, I have no intention of disrespecting anyone," Warren cut in. Then he turned back to Ben. "I'd appreciate it if we could have a word in my office."

I was so caught up in the scene that I hadn't looked at Ben's face until now. His expression was serious—too serious. The last time I'd seen that look, he had arrested the guy who tried to kill me years ago.

"No problem," Ben said. He gave Bruno a quick pat on the ears before walking toward the station.

"This is so wrong, Warren," Logan snapped. "First Dana, now Ben. Do you think I don't know what you're doing?"

Warren turned to him with a smirk that didn't suit his face—it made me want to punch him.

"I doubt you know what I'm doing, because I'm a real officer," Warren said, his tone thick with condescension. Then, to my irritation, he shifted his attention to me. "For example, you don't seem to understand that you're not allowed to get involved in this case, Forest. My case. Now, instead of wasting time here, you should be investigating this morning's incident. I'm sure Miss Willow would appreciate it. Since, you know, it's actually your job. And as impressive as Bruno is, I doubt he can solve it on his own."

My stomach dropped. "What incident?"

As Warren focused on me, his smirk disappeared. "Someone broke into the storage room behind the community center. Vandalized the place."

A chill ran down my spine.

"I told the city manager to keep it under wraps until we cleared the scene," he continued. "There was nothing you could do, Miss Willow, and I didn't want to add to your already eventful night. A robbery and a murder at the museum should be more than enough for anyone."

Although he sounded sincere, I wasn't sure whether to appreciate the gesture or be furious that I had to hear about this from him. That was *my* department. I should have been informed immediately.

Without another word, I turned on my heel and started for the exit. Then I remembered—Bruno's leash was still in my hand. He was supposed to be working with Logan now.

I turned back—and promptly collided with Logan.

Art, Vendors and Forgery

His hands caught my arms before I could stumble backward.

"Thanks," I muttered, clearing my throat and pulling away as fast as I could. I held out Bruno's leash. "Here you go."

Logan took it, frowning. I couldn't tell if it was directed at Warren, the situation, or me.

"Where are you going?" he asked, his tone calm but tight with barely concealed frustration.

"To the community center, of course."

He sighed, running a hand through his hair before brushing past me.

"Naturally, you'll be going alone," he muttered. "I suppose I'll see you there."

"This is horrible!" Terry exclaimed, not for the first time since we arrived at the Community Center. "Who would do something like this?"

I ignored the question and kept maneuvering around the piles of craft supplies, tools, and shattered wood that had once belonged to the charming festival stands Apple Creek and Maple Hollow had co-owned for as long as I could remember. It was hard to look at.

Maybe I hadn't been particularly excited about the art festival— that had always been my sister's thing. When we were kids, she was the one who took home ribbons for her "art pieces," while I got a polite nod and a pat on the back for my efforts. Personally, I never saw much of a difference between our work, but the festival had always been something my mom and Sandie shared. Eventually, I had just drifted away from it.

That didn't mean I hadn't appreciated the festival. The stands were designed to look like charming cottages, all painted in warm, matching colors. Banners hung from lampposts alongside oversized flower baskets, making everything look like something straight out of a fantasy storybook. But now, seeing it all shattered across a dim storage room—it hurt more than I expected.

"I don't even want to think about how we're going to explain this to the mayor of Maple Hollow," Terry groaned.

The mention of the mayor drained the color from Martin's face and left a pit in my stomach.

"The mayor is going to freak out," Martin muttered. "That's our mayor. I don't even want to think about the conversation with

Art, Vendors and Forgery

Maple Hollow. I mean, they might even sue us!"

"Let's try not to panic just yet," I said, making my way toward Logan, who was speaking with Harold Whitestone, the Community Center's main janitor. "Martin, have you spoken to anyone about this?"

He shook his head and let out a sigh. "Just like with you, Deputy Warren didn't want me sounding the alarm until the police had an official statement. I guess he's still focused on the museum case."

As much as I hated keeping things quiet, I could see Warren's point. I needed a plan before facing the mayor— and for that, I needed to hear what Logan had to say.

"If you remember anything else, let me know," Logan told Harold, his tone short.

Bruno, standing at attention in his official vest, took a step toward me. I resisted the urge to scratch behind his ears, knowing this was a work moment.

"I guess we're done here," Logan said, tugging lightly on Bruno's leash as he turned to leave.

"What do you mean, you're done?" I asked, stepping over broken pieces of wood to catch up. "Did you figure out what happened? Who—"

"Yes, Maggie, I've solved the entire case," he snapped, not breaking stride.

Bruno leapt gracefully over a broken stand, while I had to weave around it before jogging to catch up.

"What's wrong with you?" I asked. "Logan, what's the problem?"

Logan let out a humorless laugh, but there was no amusement in it. "Oh, I don't know, Maggie. Maybe being assigned to take statements on minor vandalism cases so my actual job gets undermined? Or maybe the fact that my former boss and mentor is being interrogated, and there's nothing I can do."

"I know it's stressful having Ben with Deputy Warren, but I'm sure he'll—"

Logan shook his head. "You know how stressful—? Maggie, you have no idea what's going on. You weren't here. You don't understand what—"

His phone rang, cutting him off. He answered immediately, his expression shifting from irritation to something darker. His knuckles went white around Bruno's leash.

"I'll be right there," he said through gritted teeth. "No, I don't care if Warren—

Art, Vendors and Forgery

well, he's about to learn not to mess with my people."

He hung up and turned for his car.

"Where are you going?" I demanded, suddenly more concerned about what he might do than where he was headed.

He spun back, his voice low but sharp. "To do my job. That's where I'm going."

I felt heat rise in my chest. "To do your job? And this isn't your job? Someone just destroyed half the festival, and you're—"

Logan leaned in, his face inches from mine. "And what exactly do you want me to do? Huh? The security footage is already on its way to the station. I've taken everyone's statements. What more do you need from me?" His voice and eyes betrayed his frustration. "I figured you wanted the police gone so you could get the festival back on track quickly. Or maybe it's you who doesn't want to do your job."

That hit me harder than it should have.

He was the one ignoring me last night. He was the one acting like I was the problem. But somehow, he had the nerve to make it about me? I stepped in closer, refusing to back down.

"You're right. I don't want to do my job. I don't want to talk to the mayor without having real answers. But this case doesn't matter to you, does it? No one died. It doesn't involve anyone you care about."

Logan's jaw tightened, but he didn't respond.

I spun around, ready to stomp back to the storage room. I hadn't expected to find Martin and Terry staring at me, their expressions filled with concern and uncertainty.

"We have a festival to fix," I said, fighting back my frustration. "Let's get busy."

Chapter 8

After only an hour, Sophie Parker—the IT girl I borrowed from Martin's department—Terry, Harold, and I had managed to clear a path through the mess. Linda had printed out a list for us to track what was missing, what needed repairs, and what had to be replaced. It was tedious work, but if I was going to save the festival, this had to be the first step.

The second step just walked through the door.

"Maggie?" Paul asked, stepping inside. It was easier now that we had cleared a path. "What happened here?"

"Paul!" I said, probably too enthusiastically, judging by the growing concern on my brother-in-law's face. "I'm so glad you're here. I need your professional help."

As I led him toward the pile of broken wooden stands and scattered supplies—screws, nails, paint cans, and who knew what else—Paul kept shaking his head.

"Were these... the festival stands?" He scratched his head. "I don't think the vendors are going to be thrilled with the new presentation."

I rolled my eyes, but his amused smile gave me hope.

"Can you fix them?"

"All of them?" His eyes widened as he took in the disaster around him.

I nodded and touched his arm. "And I need a facelift to the gazebo."

He turned to me, ready to argue, but before he could, I grinned and kept going.

"We're having live music this year. Plus, culinary arts and a bake-off."

Paul slowly started shaking his head.

"Please?" I clasped my hands together. "I don't want to be the one to tell Sandie we have to cancel the festival."

His shoulders slumped in defeat as he pulled out his phone. "I'll get the crew here, but Maggie, we'll need new supplies, and—"

Art, Vendors and Forgery

"Thank you!" I interrupted, throwing my arms around him. Somehow, things didn't seem quite so impossible anymore.

"Miss Willow?" Sophie called from the entrance. "You need to see this."

"Can't promise anything!" Paul shouted after me as I walked away.

I glanced back at him with a smile. "I know."

Paul would move mountains to make my sister happy. And thank goodness Sandie loved the arts.

Sophie had the storage inventory list in one hand and a laptop balanced on a pile of boxes in front of her. She was talking to Martin, who looked serious. Too serious.

"What is it?" I asked.

Sophie was a young intern, probably half my age, with thick glasses and a vintage sense of fashion. Her tall heels probably weren't ideal for fieldwork in the R-Parks Department, but at least she could walk in them—something I'd never mastered.

"I checked the list from Mrs. Oak, just like

you told me," she said. "I started with the most valuable items, and everything is here..." She glanced around. "Well, in some form."

"Everything?" I tried not to sound disappointed, but I kind of was. If this had been a robbery, at least it would have made sense. But pure destruction? That felt more like a protest against the festival—something I didn't want to deal with. "Are you sure?"

Sophie shifted her focus back to her laptop. "If the records are correct, I'm pretty sure."

"Once we finish cleaning up," Martin said, "we'll have a better idea of what actually needs replacing."

I scanned the room again, unease creeping in. We had a ton of paint cans, yet not a single bit of graffiti marked the warehouse walls. I supposed not all vandalism involved words or symbols, but it still felt... off.

Before I could dwell on it, my phone rang. My stomach clenched when I saw my mom's name on the screen. My first thought was Ben.

"Mom?" I answered, trying to keep my voice steady, just in case she needed something else.

I was right.

"Maggie! The police arrested Ben!"

A million thoughts flooded my mind—

most of them things I didn't want my mom to hear. Telling her I already knew he was at the station wouldn't help.

"I'm heading there right now, Mom. Stay home."

"No! I called Sandie. She's going to stay with the kids so I can—"

Paul suddenly appeared in front of me, his phone to his ear. I didn't need to ask—I could hear my sister's voice coming through the speaker.

"Mom, Paul is here with me. We'll go to the station. We are closer. I'll call you from there."

I hung up and grabbed Paul's phone from his hand.

"Sandie," I said sharply, my shift in tone enough to make her go silent. "Get to Mom and wait for me to call again."

I didn't wait for her reply. I needed to get to the station before my mom stormed in and made things worse. Logan had made it very clear that Deputy Warren wasn't like Ben or Chief Anderson. And I had a feeling he wouldn't tolerate my family's outbursts.

Chapter 9

The station was more crowded than I'd ever seen it. And considering how often I'd been here with Bruno, that was saying something.

Paul followed me straight to the service window. I expected to see Tricia, but instead, a frustrated officer—one I'd only seen a couple of times—greeted us.

"What can I do for you?"

I glanced around, still thrown by the number of people in the lobby. Paul got ahead of me and answered first.

"We're here to check on Benjamin Morales. We know he was arrested this—"

The officer sighed and gestured to the people around us. "You and everyone else here

Art, Vendors and Forgery

are trying to check on Mr. Morales. Are you family?"

Paul started to shake his head, but I gripped his arm and cut in.

"Yes. I'm his daughter."

"Daughter?" the officer raised an eyebrow.

"Stepdaughter. Adopted kind."

His eyes narrowed as he leaned in. "You know it's a crime to lie to an officer, right?"

I placed a hand over my heart and summoned all my acting skills. "Of course. Are you trying to deny me access to my father just because we aren't blood related? Isn't that discrimination?" I turned to Paul, who looked thoroughly caught off guard—though his expression actually helped my case.

"I think so..." he said, about as convincingly as Darcy swearing she'd never sneak cookies in her pajamas again.

The officer's patience snapped, and he looked about ready to arrest us when Logan's voice cut through.

"She isn't lying, Hardison."

Hardison frowned at Logan but stayed quiet.

"I mean about being Morales' daughter," Logan clarified. "Not sure about the discrimi-

73

nation part." He gave me a look—I could see he was still mad at me.

"I know Ben, and he's never mentioned a family, Forest," Hardison said.

Logan nodded, lowering his voice as he stepped closer. "Yeah, well. Who likes to talk about the things that have broken their soul?"

Hardison's posture shifted. His tension didn't vanish entirely, but his tone softened when he turned back to us.

"I'm afraid you can't see him. He's waiting for a lawyer before his bail hearing."

I opened my mouth, but Logan didn't let me speak.

"Perfect. While you wait for your adopted-stepfather's update, I need to talk to you about the Community Center case. Follow me. He can come too."

He didn't even glance at Paul before turning and walking toward his office.

Paul leaned in as we followed, muttering, "Don't you love how they ask, but it's never really a question?"

His tone made it clear—he was not happy with me.

Art, Vendors and Forgery

The second I stepped into Logan's office, Bruno leaped from his bed to greet me. After the morning I'd had, a welcoming friend was exactly what I needed. I dropped to the floor and buried my hands in his fur.

"He's working, you know," Logan said, moving to the back of his office to pull a binder from a cabinet.

Any other day, I would've jumped up and left Bruno alone. But today wasn't that day. I ignored Logan's comment and kept scratching behind Bruno's ears—because Bruno was mine now.

Paul stayed by the door, arms crossed, his expression unreadable. While things between Logan and my mom had changed drastically, his relationship with my sister—and especially my brother-in-law—had barely improved. At least they weren't fighting. Yet.

Logan dropped the binder onto his desk with a thud. "I finished the report on the vandalism case. Thought you might want to look it over before I send it to the mayor."

I stood and opened the binder. It was at least two inches thick—but inside, there were only three pages.

"That's it?" I asked, struggling to contain my frustration. "You really don't care?"

Logan shook his head, but didn't meet my eyes. "It's not that, Maggie. I shouldn't even be on this case. This is Warren's way of punishing me for... Never mind. The point is, the investigation is done. It's closed. You can move forward with the festival."

I let the binder fall shut. "I'll figure it out myself, then."

Logan chuckled, stopping me before I could storm out.

"I would've bet you'd be more interested in figuring out what's going on with Ben and the *real* crime."

I turned back, narrowing my eyes. "The real crime? The art festival may not happen and you..." I signed trying to control myself. "Of course I want to know what's going on with Ben, but—"

"Great!" Logan cut me off, crossing his arms. "Then you should know he's being accused of conspiracy and murder."

I stepped back, instinctively looking to Paul. He entered the office now, his guarded stance shifting to something closer to concern.

"Conspiracy and murder of—" I covered my mouth, pulse quickening. "The curator? How—why would they accuse him? He wasn't even there."

"Exactly!" Logan spread his arms. "Imagine my surprise when I read the witness list and saw *your* name on it."

I frowned, shaking my head.

"You were *where*?" Paul's panic was rising now. "You witnessed a murder? *Again*?"

"I didn't *witness* a murder," I shot back, then turned to Logan, pointing a finger at him. "And you know that, Logan. I've *never* witnessed a murder. Why are you acting surprised? You saw me there last night?"

Paul's head snapped toward Logan. "*You* were there too? *Again?*"

Logan ignored him. "I didn't see you, Maggie. I was there because Dana called me. She's also being accused—same charges."

"Dana?" Paul's voice dropped, almost like he was piecing something together. "Thompson? *Your* Dana?"

"She's not *my* Dana," Logan muttered, running a hand through his hair. "But yes. Dana Thompson." He exhaled, finally meeting my eyes. "I'm sorry for the accusation, but I really didn't see you last night. It was a long one."

Paul whistled, scratching the back of his neck. "That's rough, man. Especially considering... I guess you're off the case?"

Logan nodded, avoiding my eyes again.

"This is the worst time for Chief Anderson to be gone," he said. "And I don't think it's a coincidence that Ben is back now. But, of course, I *can't* talk to him."

I crossed my arms. "And you think I—we know about Ben?"

Logan shrugged, a smirk forming. "It's no secret you have a way of getting around police investigations. And since this involves your adopted-stepfather, I figured you might share what you learn."

Paul's tone shifted instantly. "You're asking Maggie to put herself in danger because you *can't*—"

"I would *never* ask Maggie to do that," Logan snapped. The tension between them flared again. "But I *won't* pretend she's going to sit this one out—especially when I can't be there to protect her."

His words sent a flicker of warmth through me—right before they hit the wrong nerve.

"I know how to tie my own shoelaces, Logan," I shot back. "And contrary to *popular belief*, I don't *enjoy* getting tangled up in police investigations."

"Great!" Logan leaned forward, resting his hands on his desk. "So, promise me you'll stay

Art, Vendors and Forgery

out of this one. Promise me you won't get involved when Ben—someone you consider *family*—is being accused by a man who was fired years ago for using questionable investigative methods. You want to guess who fired him?"

I closed my eyes, exhaling slowly. I should've known there was more to the story. Not that it would have changed anything. I wasn't about to ignore Ben, but this was really not ideal.

When I looked up, Logan was smirking again.

"So," I asked, bracing myself, "what do you propose?"

Chapter 10

Logan didn't want to talk at the station, which I completely understood. And I certainly didn't want to talk at my house—I was already dreading having to explain to my mom the little I knew about Ben's case. Paul was going to be part of the plan since no one would suspect him and Logan working together. The problem was, we still didn't know what the plan was yet.

"Margaret!"

Catherine Roberts's unmistakable voice echoed through the station just as I walked out of Logan's office. "Wait, please!"

I turned to Paul. "You better go talk to Sandie and Mom. This might take a while."

"All right, but hurry. I have to get back to

Art, Vendors and Forgery

your mess, Maggie. Those stands won't build themselves."

I gave him a quick hug before he headed out, then turned to face Catherine as she hurried toward me, weaving through the desks.

"Oh, Maggie," she gasped, throwing her arms around me and resting her head on my shoulder. Her body shook as she cried. "This is horrible! They think I killed that poor man! Are you being accused too?"

Catherine was either an excellent actress or genuinely desperate. Given the way her hands trembled as she gripped my shoulders, I was leaning toward the latter.

"Are you, Maggie?" she repeated, staring into my eyes.

I shook my head slowly, still trying to process everything. Logan hadn't mentioned Catherine being charged, too. Though he *had* said Deputy Warren had been fired for his questionable investigative methods. Three people charged in less than a day—two of them with conspiracy—seemed extreme.

"Maggie, listen to me." Catherine's voice shifted, the fear giving way to urgency. "I'm being framed, and you *have* to believe me. I would never hurt anyone. And I would *never* damage the painting." Her grip on my arms tightened. "You need to find it, please. The police here don't care about it!"

"Mrs. Roberts," a voice interrupted.

I turned to see Tricia approaching us.

"We have to go," she said firmly.

Catherine inhaled deeply, then let out a slow, controlled breath. Carefully, she wiped the bottom of her eyes before pinching her cheeks to bring some color back to her face. Then, with the grace of someone used to being in the public eye, she straightened her posture and forced a polite smile.

"If we must go..." She nodded at me. "Meet me at my house later this evening. We'll talk about the festival there."

I watched as she and Tricia crossed the lobby. A soft, familiar groan caught my attention, and I felt a furry nudge against my hand.

I looked down to find Bruno watching me, ears perked, waiting.

"What do you think, Bruno?" I crouched down and scratched behind his ears. "You *are* an officer here. Any thoughts?"

"Mom," I called as I stepped inside the house.

Art, Vendors and Forgery

Darcy ran from the kitchen and threw her arms around me. Her warm hug was exactly what I needed after the long day. I squeezed her tight, appreciating the moment more than she knew.

"Where's Grandma, sunflower?"

Darcy pointed toward the kitchen. "She's in the backyard with Aunt Sandie." Then, lowering her voice, she added, "I think she's crying, but she doesn't want me or Toby to see. Is everything okay, Mommy?"

I knelt down, tucking her hair behind her ear while keeping my voice as calm as possible. "Remember Ben? Grandma's just worried about him."

"Is he sick?" Darcy's eyes widened. "Maybe we can bring him some soup or ice cream! Logan hasn't come over yet, so we still have the rainbow one."

The deck door creaked open, and I heard my mom and Sandie talking as they walked inside.

"He's not sick, but I'm sure he'd love some soup or ice cream when we get to see him," I said, smiling at her attempt to help. "Who do you think got Grandma so obsessed with clam chowder?"

Darcy giggled, but I could still see the

worry in her eyes. It weighed on me—I needed to figure this out. Fast.

As I stood, I took in my mom's face. Darcy was right. She'd been crying, and the worry she carried was impossible to hide.

"Did Paul tell you—"

"He called," Sandie cut in, "but he didn't say much. Or make much sense. Did you ask him to rebuild the festival stands?"

I kissed Darcy on the forehead and walked into the kitchen. If I were being honest, I'd nearly forgotten about the vandalism at the storage room. Luckily, Paul hadn't.

Yeah, someone trashed a storage room at the Community Center. Strangely, nothing appears to be missing. Anyway, Paul's helping rebuild the stands so we can have the festival.... or at least return them in good shape to Maple Hollow. Martin doesn't need another incident."

Mom let out a heavy sigh and sank onto a stool. "Just what we need—another crime tied to this family."

I glanced at Darcy, whose smile had vanished completely.

"No crime in this family, Mom," I said quickly, and though I still didn't like how Logan handled the case, in that moment I felt relieved. "Logan already closed the case. Now we just need to get back on track for the art festival, which, by the way, is in two weeks, and we're as behind as we were yesterday."

Although my words didn't seem to reassure my mom, they were enough to ease Darcy's mind. Before Mom could respond, I sent Darcy to look for Toby. I wasn't sure where my nephew was, but I didn't want her in the kitchen for this conversation. She already had enough questions, and I knew they'd come pouring out at bedtime.

Once she was outside, I turned back to my family.

"Paul and I talked to Logan," I said.

Sandie raised a brow. "Paul talked to Logan?" She slid onto the stool next to Mom. "Things must be really bad if my Paul—"

"Sandie, really?" I shot her a look, but Mom waved a dismissive hand, urging me to continue.

"What did Logan say?"

Now came the hard part.

"Apparently, Ben is being charged with conspiracy and murder. A museum curator was killed last night."

Sandie covered her mouth to stifle a gasp,

but it was my mom's silence that sent a chill down my spine.

"He's not the only one," I continued. "Deputy Warren is also charging Mrs. Roberts and Dana Thompson."

"That must be rough for Logan," Sandie said. "Sure, she's his ex-wife, but that doesn't mean he's over her, right? I mean, if Andrew got arrested, you'd be really concerned, wouldn't you?"

I wasn't sure what bothered me more—her mentioning Andrew or the fact that she apparently knew more about Logan's life than I did. Either way, I ignored her and pushed forward.

"I'm meeting with Mrs. Roberts this evening to see what she knows. I don't know if I'll be able to talk to Ben yet."

Mom buried her face in her hands. "Ben needs a lawyer. A good one. Do you think Andrew could send one?"

I blinked at her, caught completely off guard. "Andrew? Why would you—"

"He had a friend," she interrupted. "Remember? The one he called when you got caught up in that case over spring break?"

I took a step back. "That was years ago! I don't even know if Andrew still talks to that friend. What we need to do is figure out—"

"No, Margaret!" Mom's voice was sharp as she stood. "You are not getting involved in this. I won't let you end up needing a lawyer, too."

I reached for her hand. "Mom, you don't have to worry about me. I'm fine. No one is accusing me of anything. But according to Logan—"

I had planned to leave out the part about Warren, but apparently my mom already knew about it.

"Deputy Warren is no friend to Ben or Logan," her voice low and firm. "You weren't here, but I was. I don't trust that man. And the last thing I want is for Warren to find an excuse to use you to punish Ben even more."

I turned to Sandie, but she suddenly found the kitchen wall fascinating, refusing to meet my gaze.

"What happened?" I asked.

Mom straightened, her tone leaving no room for argument. "What we're going to do is find Ben a lawyer. If you don't want to call Andrew, fine. But you will do nothing else. I hope I'm making myself very clear."

Without waiting for a response, she stormed upstairs, leaving me with more questions than answers—along with a deepening worry for both Ben and Logan.

Chapter 11

Sandie decided everyone needed a distraction, so she took Toby and Darcy to the splash pad. I wanted to go with her, but it was Wednesday, and technically, I was still working. So, I drove back to the Community Center instead.

Terry and Sophie were still sorting out the mess, and I was relieved to see Paul's truck along with at least two other guys working around the scattered pieces of wood. If my mom didn't want me looking into Ben's case, I would do my best to stay away. That didn't mean I wouldn't meet with Logan later, but first, I needed to warn Paul about the developments at the house.

As I walked toward him, Sophie noticed me and waved, so I changed directions.

Art, Vendors and Forgery

"Miss Willow," she greeted me. "I believe we've finished sorting everything, and aside from the stands, everything was just out of place."

"What do you mean?" I asked. Terry answered instead, excitement creeping into his voice.

"It means we can keep going with the festival! Everything is here—the supplies, the tools, even the few items some of the vendors had already dropped off."

"The flower baskets and the lamps?" I asked because I thought those delicate items might have been ruined.

Terry smiled widened as he nodded.

I was relieved but confused. Why go through the trouble of wrecking the entire storage room to only break the stands? I knew it wasn't a robbery, but it didn't feel like simple vandalism either.

"Are you sure nothing is missing? Broken?"

Terry cleared his throat. "Well, aside from the stands, but Paul found all the pieces. Looks like we only need to replace a few."

"That's very..." I bit my tongue, keeping my suspicions to myself. "Those are great news. I'll check in with Paul about the stands so we can move forward with the planning."

Paul was talking to one of his guys when I approached. It was incredible how, in just a few hours, what had seemed like a lost cause of wooden beams and fallen signs was starting to look like an actual project that just might be finished in time.

"You made it back," Paul said, stepping around some scattered materials. "I talked to Sandie. Your mom won't be happy if we get involved with Logan or the police."

"I know. We shouldn't." I ignored the questioning look he gave me. "What's the update?"

I gestured around the storage room.

"We should have everything fixed by Monday. Wednesday if it rains."

I turned to him, skeptical. "Are you sure? It looked terrible this morning."

Paul straightened with a grin. "We're pretty good at fixing things. Besides, it wasn't that bad after all."

"What do you mean?" I asked, feeling some of my earlier stress ease.

"Most of the stuff was just disassembled and scattered. I only needed to replace a couple of beams for two of the stands."

Something didn't sit right. "Which stands?"

Paul scratched his head. "Not sure. The

Art, Vendors and Forgery

numbers on them were 11 and 6, but I don't know if they had vendors assigned yet. I've never done the art festival setup before."

I patted his shoulder. "Well, this is your lucky year. Anything else strike you as strange?"

"Strange?" he echoed, frowning. "Like what?"

"Something that doesn't make sense. Something unexpected."

Paul smirked. "You sound like a detective, Maggie."

I playfully punched his arm. "That's not what I'm doing. I just want to figure out what happened so it doesn't happen again."

"Got it, got it!" He held up his hands in surrender. "Now that you mention it..." He trailed off, staring toward the far wall, his mouth pressing into a thin line.

"What is it?"

He hesitated, then sighed. "It's weird that there's no graffiti. I figured they didn't have time, but then I found the paint supply. All the spray cans were unopened and full. If someone was here to make a mess, why not use them?"

I raised an eyebrow. "Something Sandie needs to know about your late night hobbies?"

"Very funny, Margaret. Anyway, the only

opened box was acrylics—one bottle was missing."

"Acrylic paint?" I followed his gaze as he pointed to a nearby table.

"Yeah, like the kind Toby uses at school, but bigger. There was an empty space in the box, but no signs of paint anywhere."

"City staff hasn't been working in here, have they? Why would anyone take just one bottle of acrylic paint?"

Paul shrugged. "Sometimes we use it for minor touch-ups on the stands. It's normal to have craft paint around."

That made sense, but it still felt off. "Thanks, Paul."

I turned to leave, but he called after me.

"You're going to see Logan, aren't you? Against your mom's wishes?"

I tilted my head. He wasn't wrong. My mom was firm in her decision, but I wasn't sure if it was a good idea to back off completely.

I smiled. "We're going to talk to Logan."

"We?" Paul crossed his arms. "I don't think I should be part of this."

"We're just telling him we changed our minds because of Mom."

"Nope. Call him. That'll save a trip."

Art, Vendors and Forgery

I shrugged. "I have to pick up Bruno, anyway. And food sounds good about now."

Paul groaned. "Fine. I'll go. But just for the food. And maybe for your dog. Toby loves him."

"Thanks!" I took a few steps backward, keeping my eyes on him. "Meet me at the tavern."

Paul shook his head, but I cut him off before he could argue.

"Sorry! I need to talk to Mrs. Roberts. She's under house arrest or something. Just order some chips for me, will you?"

As I turned to leave, I heard him shout, "You're just like your sister!"

I just smiled.

Mrs. Roberts' home was just outside Apple Creek, one of those sprawling mansions that made you wonder what purpose so many rooms could possibly serve. As I pulled into the long driveway, I spotted her already waiting at the entrance, her figure tense against the glow of the porch lights.

"Margaret! Thank goodness you're here!"

She practically yanked me into a hug the second I stepped out of my car. But as quickly as she embraced me, she pulled back, smoothing the front of her blouse as though she'd just caught herself making a mistake.

"Please, come in. And... forgive my sensitivity. It has been a long, horrible day."

"Don't apologize," I reassured her, following her through the grand foyer. "It hasn't been an easy day for anyone."

She offered me a smile, but it was thin, barely holding back the worry that darkened her features.

The house was just as elegant as I'd imagined—perfectly matched wallpaper and furniture, crystal chandeliers, and at least three sitting rooms we passed on our way down a hallway. She led me into what could have passed for a library, though the warmth of the décor made it feel more personal.

"I'm glad you're staying out of this mess, Margaret," she said as she gestured for me to sit. "I just don't understand it. Who could possibly think I could kill anyone?"

I opened my mouth to ask what she meant, but she let out a breathy sigh and sank into the chair across from me, rubbing her temples.

Art, Vendors and Forgery

"I wish I knew!" she said, her voice breaking slightly. "Deputy Warren said it was suspicious—how insistent I was about seeing Tristan last night. But I got that email! The one from the Historical Preservation that I told you about it. Or at least, I thought it was from them..."

I frowned. "You thought?"

Mrs. Roberts lifted her head, her face pale. "The deputy says the email came from a ghost account, not the foundation. They think I made the whole thing up."

"But even if it was a fake account," I said slowly, "that would still explain why you were so concerned about the painting."

She let out a bitter laugh and shook her head. "He thinks I'm putting on an act. He doesn't understand how important that painting is. Apple Creek deserves a proper art museum, Margaret! A real one! How are we supposed to keep our artists here if we don't give them a place to shine? They all leave for the city."

Something about the way she said it made me pause. There was something more—something implied beneath her words—but I wasn't sure if it had anything to do with the murder or just her own frustrations.

Montie Red

Before I could ask, a woman entered the room carrying a tray with a delicate tea set. The scent of chamomile and honey drifted through the air, reminding me of home.

"Thank you, Paula," Mrs. Roberts said, barely glancing at the woman. "I'll take it from here."

Paula shot me a tight, apologetic smile before scurrying out of the room, looking relieved to be excused. I couldn't blame her. It had been a long day for everyone in this house, and the tension was thick enough to choke on.

"If I remember correctly," Mrs. Roberts mused, stirring her tea absentmindedly, "your mother, Lucretia, is quite fond of tea. Years ago, at one of Mrs. Gladis' gatherings, she brought the most marvelous mixture. I never got the chance to ask her about it. Maybe I'll speak with her one of these days... well, once I'm allowed to leave my home again."

She let out a humorless chuckle, but there was a flicker of something raw in her eyes.

I reached across the table, giving her hand a gentle squeeze. "It'll all be resolved soon, Catherine."

She nodded, but the doubt in her expression mirrored my own.

My mother's words echoed in my head as I

Art, Vendors and Forgery

found myself asking, "What makes people think I can figure these things out?"

Mrs. Roberts let out a soft chuckle. "Well, you did uncover that conspiracy against the city not too long ago. My husband hasn't stopped talking about it."

Of course. I hadn't even thought about the fact that Mr. Roberts, our city council member, was married to the woman sitting in front of me.

"I didn't do much," I said, feeling my cheeks warm slightly. "Honestly, it was my lack of information that helped me stumble onto the truth."

Mrs. Roberts tilted her head, watching me with an unreadable expression. "Investigation," she corrected. "You helped the police with an investigation. And you figured it out."

I took a sip of my tea, using it as an excuse to avoid her knowing gaze.

So far, according to Mrs. Roberts, she had received an email—one that supposedly came from that foundation but was later deemed fake. A little too convenient. That must have been why Deputy Warren considered it suspicious. I had to admit, her insistence on having the painting at the festival was unusual. And now, with the artist's death increasing the painting's value, the situation looked even worse for her.

That said, looking around at the luxury surrounding me, I couldn't see why money would be her motive.

"Can I see the email?" I asked.

Catherine sighed, shaking her head. "The police have my phone and computer. I don't want to risk checking my email and giving Deputy Warren more reason to think I'm part of some conspiracy."

I leaned back, disappointed but understanding. "And what exactly is this supposed conspiracy?"

"It's the most ridiculous accusation I've ever heard," a new voice cut in.

I turned just as Mr. Roberts entered the room, his expression tight with frustration. "And I've worked in Apple Creek's city council for years," he added.

He placed a reassuring hand on Mrs. Roberts' shoulder. She leaned into his touch slightly, and just like that, some of her tension seemed to ease.

I watched them for a second, something about the quiet moment between them making me feel oddly envious.

"I can understand how the accusation

sounds vague," I admitted. "But Deputy Warren must have a reason for an arrest, right?"

Mr. Roberts let out a loud sigh, raising a skeptical eyebrow at his wife. "How much does she know, Catherine? Did you show her the studio?"

Chapter 12

Mr. Roberts flipped on the light, and my eyes wandered up the tall walls of a room on the far side of the house. Every surface was filled with striking artwork.

"This is my sweet Catherine's pride and joy," he said.

Mrs. Roberts' face lit up as she walked slowly into the room, her fingers brushing the air near the canvases like she was greeting old friends. I didn't know where to look first. The collection ranged from vivid landscapes to surreal, color-drenched abstracts. Each painting was framed in dark, beautifully carved wood that probably cost as much as the art itself.

"I've always loved fine art," she said, pausing in the center of the room. "Once upon

Art, Vendors and Forgery

a time, I dreamed of becoming an artist whose work would hang in galleries... but I didn't have the skill."

"That's not true," Mr. Roberts said, lowering himself into one of the large chairs and glancing at me. "These may be works from other artists, but my Catherine has pieces of her own all around the house."

Her face flushed, and she waved a hand as if brushing his words away. "Those are just little craft projects."

"Crafting?" he echoed, then scoffed. "Once you leave this room, Miss Willow, take a good look at the walls. They're remarkable."

I couldn't help but smile at the pride in his voice. "I'll be sure to look closely, Mr. Roberts."

But Mrs. Roberts wasn't in the mood for flattery. She turned toward me, her voice rising with urgency. "I promise you, Margaret, I didn't invite you here to admire amateur paintings. This—" she gestured around the room, "—is why Deputy Warren thinks I conspired with Dana to steal the Rodriguez."

Even to my untrained eye, the collection was valuable. I knew Sebastian Rodriguez was a respected artist of our time, but I doubted his painting could eclipse the pieces in this room.

"Just because you have an art collection?"

Mr. Roberts cleared his throat and gave his wife a stern look. Catherine suddenly found her intertwined fingers very interesting.

"Oh, Catherine," he said with a groan, leaning forward. "Of course it's not just that. But my wife's admiration for Rodriguez has never been subtle. And then there are the emails with Miss Thompson... it doesn't look good."

"I didn't mean anything by them—especially not to involve poor Dana," Mrs. Roberts said, her voice cracking slightly. "I was frustrated with Tristan for refusing to feature the Rodriguez. He's our local artist, and yet half of Apple Creek doesn't even know who he is, Margaret!"

She had a point. Most residents only went to the museum on school field trips, and even then, the focus was on local history, not art. I'd always wondered why it was called the *History and Art* Museum in the first place.

"But that's not the issue," Mr. Roberts continued. "Deputy Warren believes Catherine conspired with Dana to steal the painting. And the murder? Supposedly an unfortunate escalation."

"That makes no sense," Catherine said, exasperated. "I've said it before—to you and the mayor—I only wanted the painting recognized for what it was. I never wanted to take it. And certainly not to hurt Scott!"

"Scott?" I asked, surprised. "You knew the curator?"

She nodded, a troubled look in her eyes. "Yes, and I was shocked when I found out he was doing the appraisal. He specialized in historical artifacts, not fine art. But Tristan seemed satisfied—he and Scott were close friends." She turned to her husband, her hand covering her mouth. "Oh my. Tristan must be shocked."

Her concern sounded genuine, and while I hated to press, I had to ask, "Do you know how Scott died?"

Mrs. Roberts leaned against her husband, shaking her head. He answered for her.

"The police are still waiting on the medical examiner's report. If it was a heart attack, all of this might blow over."

"But what about the painting?" Catherine asked, her voice tight with anxiety. "Will they just forget it was stolen?"

"They already found it, Catherine."

Both of us stared at him.

"It was discovered in Dana's office," he

said, then turned to me. "Please, keep this between us. I know about it because of my position on the council. Warren is trying to keep it quiet."

"Of course," I said. "You have my word. Do you know anything else?"

He sighed, the lines on his face softening. "Not much. But... it's believed that our former chief, Ben Morales, might have been involved."

My heart stopped for a moment.

"I'm sorry, Miss Willow," he added gently. "I know how close he was to your mother. And again—it may have just been a heart attack. Maybe Dana was trying to protect the painting. Who knows?"

He didn't finish the thought, and I appreciated that. I didn't believe Ben could have killed anyone—especially not for a piece of art. But something in this house wasn't adding up. I had a lot more information now... and even more questions.

"Will you help me, Margaret?" Mrs. Roberts asked suddenly, standing and walking toward me. "I don't trust this deputy. Fred hasn't mentioned it, but they've had a difficult history. I'm afraid his judgment might be... compromised."

Mr. Roberts stood as well, and the

Art, Vendors and Forgery

warmth in his face vanished. "If he's holding a grudge, he's making a serious mistake. I signed off on his dismissal for good reason. And I opposed his return when Anderson brought him back—because I haven't seen any sign that he's changed. I hope he proves me wrong."

As I walked out of the house, I paid more attention to the paintings on the walls. Mr. Roberts was right—most of them were lovely pieces, filled with happy scenes and colorful landscapes. But then, out of the corner of my eye, through a half-open door, I noticed one that looked strangely familiar.

My distraction didn't go unnoticed. Mrs. Roberts caught my glance and quietly motioned for me to follow her into the room where the painting was hanging.

"It isn't as pretty as the original," she said, lingering by the door, "but it's still a magnificent copy."

There it was—the Sebastian Rodriguez painting that had supposedly been stolen and later found in Dana's office. The one Mrs.

Roberts had spoken about with such passion. It was right in front of me.

"Please, take a closer look," she said gently. "You'll see it isn't the same. The sky... that strange blue—it's not quite the same tone."

I stepped closer as she reached in and flicked on the light. She was right. It wasn't the same painting. Not exactly.

"You see, Sebastian painted the original first," she explained. "Then he went back and made a copy—just like many artists do. He only made two of this kind, though. I acquired this one many years ago. You can see the serial number at the bottom. That big red '2 of 2'—there it is."

Unlike the other art pieces she proudly displayed, Mrs. Roberts didn't seem happy or even particularly fond of this one. She barely looked at it, and stayed near the doorway, as far from the painting as she could.

"But isn't this still considered owning a Rodriguez?" I asked, genuinely curious.

She chuckled and reached to turn off the light, signaling that my time in the room was done.

"Hardly, sweetie. This is more like a handmade lithograph. Just a crafty imitation of the

Art, Vendors and Forgery

original. And let's be honest—it's not even his best copy."

I had noticed the differences, just as she'd promised. The sky in this version was darker, more brooding—less like a calm day and more like a brewing storm.

Funny thing was, I liked it more.

The original had a nice shade of blue, sure, but that was it. This one—the copy—made me feel something. Just like art was supposed to do, or so Sandie always said.

Chapter 13

"Finally!" Paul shouted as he walked toward me from the tavern entrance. "What took you so long? I was about to kill myself. I think only Bruno is having a good time."

I glanced at the large beer in his hand. "You look like you're doing just fine."

Paul scoffed. "Are you nuts? It's terrifying —just thinking what your sister will do to me if I have another one of these. It's only Wednesday, and she's already in distress with your mom. Remember?"

I rolled my eyes and looked around. As expected, the place was packed, even for a weeknight. But the smell drifting from the kitchen made it easy to understand why people would want to escape midweek monotony.

"Where's Bruno?"

Paul groaned and headed into the tavern, motioning for me to follow. "Your friend sent him to the kitchen. Said it was too crowded. I think his company didn't like the fur."

I followed him to the back where booths lined the wall. It only took a few steps to spot Logan. His back was to me, but he was tall enough to be visible over the seat. Then I saw who he was talking to—and a wave of unease twisted in my gut.

"Now, be nice," Paul whispered, stepping ahead of me with a fake smile. "Like me."

He slid into the booth without hesitation, pushing Dana slightly in the process. Her face curled into a scowl.

"I'm not sitting next to *him*, and *you* chose this seat," Paul said, gesturing to the spot in front of him.

Logan glanced up, catching my eye, then moved aside to make room. But before I could sit, Dana huffed, pushed Paul out with surprising force, and shoved past me—her shoulder brushing mine harder than it needed to—so she could slide in next to Logan.

"Better," she said with a frown at Paul.

A chuckle and a bit too much politeness accompanied my clever brother-in-law's gesture toward the seat. "After you, Maggie. Sharing this luxurious space with such a wonderful person is fine by me."

The booth suddenly felt much smaller.

The tension wasn't just about the case. Paul had hinted at something earlier, but now I was beginning to understand. Whatever had happened between Dana and Logan—it wasn't over. And from the look she gave me, I wasn't exactly welcome.

I didn't like how things ended with Andrew, but I was sure we could at least sit through dinner civilly. This? This felt loaded.

"Thanks for coming, Maggie," Logan said, his voice quieter than usual.

Dana immediately exhaled sharply and crossed her arms.

Logan ignored her. "Paul mentioned you were with Mrs. Roberts?"

I opened my mouth, but Dana cut in before I could get a word out.

"That *crazy* woman is the one who did it!"

Logan turned to her, frowning. "Dana, you have to stop. You don't know—"

"But I *do*, Logan," she snapped, leaning forward. "She'll agree with me." She pointed at me like I was a prop.

"I'm not sure why you think I would—"

Art, Vendors and Forgery

"Oh come on, *Margaret*," Dana said, pointedly using my full name. "She's been sending *hundreds* of emails—to all of us. The mayor, Director DeVoir, the museum board. There's no way she's been reasonable with you. She's trying to sabotage the whole festival!"

As much as I wanted Dana to be wrong, I had been worried about Mrs. Roberts' insistence on the painting. But the more I get to know the council member's wife, the more it felt... well, normal. Eccentric, yes—but not dangerous. Unlike Dana who, if Mr. Roberts had told me the truth, was plainly lying to all of us.

"She hasn't been unreasonable—"

"Really?" Dana increased her sarcastic tone. "Most likely, she stashed the painting away in her massive home."

To my surprise, it was Paul who jumped in next.

"And what does Ben have to do with all this, Dana?"

Dana's expression faltered. The righteous fury drained from her face, replaced by something much harder to read. Guilt? She slid her hands under the table and didn't respond.

Logan sighed and rested his forearms on the table. "As far as I know, the police found

111

something from Ben's wallet near the body." He looked at me, and I caught the fear behind his eyes—the same fear I saw the last time he was accused of murder.

"I don't have many details, but it doesn't make sense. Paul's right. I don't understand the connection between Dana, Mrs. Roberts, and Ben."

I kept my mouth shut. I trusted Logan, even if things between us were complicated. Paul had no clue about any of the undercurrents, but Dana—well, she clearly had her own agenda.

The speed with which she pinned everything on Mrs. Roberts made me uneasy. According to Mr. Roberts, the painting had been found in her office. Maybe she didn't know it was there, but I wasn't about to bet on that.

"Did your mom say anything?" Dana asked suddenly. "I bet Ben knew that woman. She has money, and he used to be our police chief. It seems fishy that he just showed up—"

"Are you implying Ben killed that man?" Logan's voice was sharp. Sharper than I'd heard in a while. The threat in it wasn't subtle.

Paul cleared his throat and cut through the rising tension.

Art, Vendors and Forgery

"Ben is innocent. And no, Maggie's mom didn't say anything," he said, setting his beer down and standing. "Actually, she did say something. She doesn't want any of us getting more involved in this case. So, Forest, we're leaving."

I opened my mouth to protest, but Logan beat me to it.

"Of course." He stood as well and offered his hand to Paul, who hesitated for a second but then shook it.

"Thanks for dealing with all of this," Logan said, glancing subtly over his shoulder at Dana. I wasn't supposed to notice, but I did. So did Paul, apparently, because a crooked smile tugged at his lips.

"No problem," Paul said, turning to me. "I'll see you at your mom's. Drive safe."

"Maggie," Logan said gently, like he was still wrestling with whether to say more. But instead, he just reminded me, "Don't forget Bruno. He's in the kitchen with Mr. Elliot—probably eating everything he's not supposed to. Sorry about that."

I smiled at him and headed to the kitchen, ignoring Dana. After a day like this, a detour with Mr. Elliot—and my very spoiled dog—sounded just about perfect.

The tavern's kitchen stirred a mix of memories in me. Back in high school, I used to meet Sandie and her friends at a small table tucked in the corner. Logan's parents still ran the place back then, and he was dating Sandie's best friend, Lucy.

It was also the same kitchen where I'd nearly been killed by a corrupt bartender—back when Logan was framed for murder.

I didn't have to look long to find Bruno. He sat perfectly still, tail wagging slowly, as Mr. Elliot "accidentally" dropped slices of grilled meat to the floor beside him. I had to hand it to him—Mr. Elliot made it look natural, but I doubted those juicy strips had simply fallen off the cutting board.

"Mr. Elliot," I said.

His face lit up with a warm smile. "Maggie! Always a pleasure. This guy..." He nodded toward Bruno and shook his head. "Bottomless pit, I swear."

I laughed and gave Bruno a scratch behind the ears. He stayed seated, staring at the counter just above eye level, hopeful as ever.

Art, Vendors and Forgery

"I'll take him home now," I said. "Before he eats your whole kitchen."

"Good call. But wait—I've got something for you."

He motioned for me to follow him to a quieter corner of the kitchen, then handed me a large paper bag.

"Careful," he said. "The soup's still hot. The pie's on the bottom. Fries might not be crispy anymore, but they should still taste pretty good."

The warm scent of creamy soup rose from the bag and reminded me just how long it had been since I'd eaten. "You are a saint," I murmured. "This is heaven."

He folded his arms and gave me a proud look. "There should be enough for you and your mom. The pie's mostly for your little one, though. Chocolate—her favorite, right?"

"That it is," I said with a soft smile.

Mr. Elliot surprised me by walking me all the way to my car. It was unusual, especially with how busy the tavern was. After I set the bag in the passenger seat and opened the back for Bruno, he stepped in close and lowered his voice.

"I've got a message for you, Maggie."

Something in his tone made me still.

"Logan asked me to tell you he didn't plan on bringing Dana tonight. He wanted to talk to you alone. Says he's hoping he can meet with you tomorrow morning. Your office."

The flicker of relief that ran through me was too quick to hide. Mr. Elliot noticed—of course he did—and gave me a knowing look.

"Then it's settled," he said kindly. "I'll let him know. Bright and early."

He turned to go, then paused. "Have a good night, Maggie. I know things will work out. You and Logan—your heads together? Ben's lucky. Very lucky."

And just like that, he stomped back inside, vanishing into the warmth and bustle of the kitchen. I barely managed a "goodnight" before the door swung shut behind him—leaving me alone with my questions, a hot bag of food, and the unsettling hope that tomorrow might bring some answers.

Chapter 14

Logan was waiting in the parking lot of City Hall. As soon as I pulled in, he walked straight to my window. His eyes looked tired, and his beard had darkened into a rough shadow.

"Sorry, Maggie," he said. "Can we talk somewhere else?"

It wasn't the seriousness of his face that worried me—it was the frustration in his voice. He didn't even wait for me to move Bruno to the back seat. He just opened the rear door and slid in, like he couldn't be bothered with protocol.

From the mirror, I watched him stare out the window, lost in thought.

"Do you want to grab breakfast?" I asked,

then added, "Or just something small if you already ate?"

He frowned and took a beat too long to answer. "Did you already eat?"

It was such a simple question. But in that moment, it felt heavier—like my answer would steer the rest of the conversation into territory I wasn't sure I wanted to tread.

"I... yeah. Yes," I said quickly.

He nodded, barely. "Then do you mind if we talk somewhere... less public?"

From behind me, I heard him exhale sharply.

"I don't want people to see us talking."

That caught me off guard. Curious? Yes. A little suspicious? Maybe. But definitely curious.

I called Linda first. She didn't love hearing I wouldn't be in the office, but sounded relieved when I said I was checking the setup for the festival. Then I rang Paul, who was just leaving his house. I asked him to start bringing the stands to the park—I'd meet him there later. That bought me a couple of hours.

Central Park was a favorite in Apple Creek. Not the sprawling kind like in New York City, but ours had charm. The Apple Creek River ran through it, and on weekends you could rent kayaks and canoes or fish from one of the wooden decks. There were three nature-themed playgrounds and shaded trails that wove through the trees like storybook paths.

My favorite part, though, was the gazebo at the center—where all the trails met. That's where the festival would take place. Easy access to parking, lots of benches, and a thick canopy of trees that kept the sun in check.

Logan didn't say much as we walked. He stayed close but silent, his thoughts clearly tangled. We reached the first bench and sat. He leaned forward, resting his head in his hands, eyes fixed on the ground.

It hurt to see him like that—haunted and worn—but not knowing what was wrong hurt more.

I gently placed a hand on his shoulder. He patted it, then finally looked at me.

"Sorry to mess up your day," he said quietly. "I promised I wouldn't do that anymore, and... here I am."

"You didn't mess up anything," I said with a sigh. Then I hesitated, choosing my words. "What happened with Deputy Warren? Years ago."

Logan sat up, still looking straight ahead. "Do you remember Officer Collins?"

My stomach tightened. George Collins.

The corrupt cop who'd nearly ruined Logan's life—and nearly ended mine. He and Matthew Jones still made regular appearances in my nightmares.

"Hard to forget him."

Logan's jaw tightened, his voice dropping. "Warren was friends with him. I didn't know back then, but they were in the academy together. When I joined the force, Warren made it clear he wasn't thrilled about it. He claimed my friendship with Ben was how I earned my title. And as I got better at my job... well, he believes I've achieved nothing without help. It's all been nepotism."

I turned slightly to watch him, even though his eyes stayed on the trees in the distance.

"After Collins got convicted, Chief Morales kept an eye on Warren. No one ever accused him of being involved in Collins' schemes, but trust... well, that's a fragile thing. People stopped believing in him. He didn't take that well."

Logan's tone grew heavier. "He got more aggressive—during arrests, during interrogations. Less patient. More desperate to prove people guilty. I thought maybe he was just trying to prove himself. I got it. I was trying to

Art, Vendors and Forgery

earn trust too. After all, I'd helped take one of our own down."

I pressed my lips together. I wanted to argue, to remind him that *he* wasn't the one who caused that mess—but I didn't interrupt.

"One night," he continued, "I was called to a scene. I remember thinking how strange it was—so dark in the middle of town. Turns out Warren had ordered the power cut. Thought it'd give us the element of surprise. It didn't. The people inside... they weren't criminals. Just a young couple who'd just moved to town."

He dragged a hand through his hair. "Warren lost it. Started screaming, accusing them. The guy was already down when I got there. I had to pull Warren off him."

He looked up at me then, pain written all over his face.

"Chief Morales was furious. So was the mayor. The council got calls all night from angry residents. Warren was fired. I got promoted."

He said it flatly, like the words tasted sour in his mouth.

"I can see how Warren might be out for revenge," I said slowly. "But do you really think he's behind this? Framing Ben? I know Ben, Logan. He's innocent. He *has* to be."

Logan frowned. This time, he reached for my hands and held them tightly.

"I'm with you. Ben couldn't have done it. I don't even think Dana could. But—I doubt Warren's involved."

I opened my mouth to ask about his reasoning, but he gripped my hands tighter.

"I know his methods are over the top, and yeah, he arrested more people than anyone else during an investigation. But after he was fired..."

Logan cleared his throat and lowered his voice.

"Only Chief Morales and I know this—Warren took it on himself to help that couple. Quietly. He paid for their medical bills. Helped fix their house. We only found out because Council member Roberts wanted to start a fund for victims and learned someone had already covered it."

I narrowed my eyes. "That shows guilt. Not that he doesn't still hate you—or Ben."

Logan leaned closer. His voice dropped to a whisper that sent a chill straight down my spine.

"Maybe. But if he really felt that guilty, would he go steal art and murder someone just to get revenge on the people who *already* got him fired? Perhaps someone is exploiting Warren's past to keep the painting?"

Before I could respond, a voice shouted from down the trail.

"Miss Willow! Miss Willow!"

We both turned. The mayor was hurrying toward us, looking unusually frazzled.

"Miss Willow, I went to your office and Mrs. Oak told me you were by the festival setup," Mayor Dostal said, wiping invisible sweat from his forehead and catching his breath. "I have to say, she's not happy with you. Apparently, you have a ton of papers to sign."

I nodded, already picturing Linda buried under towers of folders, steam probably coming out of her ears. She had every right to be mad at me.

"Mayor Dostal, have you met Detective Logan Forest?"

Logan stood and offered his hand. The mayor shook it, squinting slightly, trying to place him. I could practically see the Rolodex spinning in his mind.

"Detective Forest was in charge of Council Member Hudson's murder," I supplied.

"Of course!" the mayor exclaimed, shaking Logan's hand again with renewed enthusiasm. "Thank you for solving that case so quickly. I hope you can do the same with this one."

Logan tilted his head slightly, eyes flicking from me to the mayor. "Which case are you referring to?"

"Who should be our next chief of police, of course!" The mayor threw up his hands like the answer was obvious. "I called Morales, but, well... he needs to clear his name first. And I can't work with Warren. That man is just... I don't know... too bossy?"

I chuckled at that word. To me, that was the perfect description.

"Miss Willow, is this why..." His grin stretched wider and his whole posture seemed to loosen with relief, which only sent my anxiety spiking. "You're so clever! I knew you'd help me with this problem."

I didn't even get a chance to clarify before he was practically bouncing on his heels, steamrolling ahead.

"Detective Forest should be our chief! At least an interim chief while Morales is on leave. You're brilliant not to suggest it outright—let-

Art, Vendors and Forgery

ting me connect the dots myself? Genius! I'm glad you two are already working on festival security. We don't need another act of vandalism."

"Mr. Mayor, I really can't take the position," Logan said, raising a hand in protest. "I don't have the—"

"Modesty! So admirable." The mayor waved him off. "But in my experience, you're an excellent detective. And it's only temporary. I wouldn't want to pull a great officer off the street for good. Paperwork is what kills us."

"Mr. Mayor, it's an honor, but—"

"Say no more, Detective Forest! You're the answer Apple Creek needs. Even Roberts will approve. He's not thrilled with Warren either. Finally, something we agree on!"

He turned on his heel and shouted over his shoulder, "I'll make the announcement tonight at the meeting!"

As I watched the mayor disappear down the path, Logan gently nudged my arm.

"What?" I asked, playing innocent.

"You could've stopped him. I *can't* take that position, Maggie. There's protocol. I'm not even in the running for chief."

I smirked and tilted my head. "So humble."

"Maggie! This isn't the time." He crossed

his arms, clearly frustrated. "What about Ben? The murder?"

"Well," I said, brushing a leaf off my shoulder, "as chief, you'd have access to everything, wouldn't you?"

Logan narrowed his eyes and leaned in until we were nose to nose. "Warren's going to lose it. You know that, right? I might actually get murdered."

I opened my mouth to joke, but stopped. He was right. This wasn't just a promotion—it was a powder keg.

"Okay, let's forget the mayor—for now. What do we *know* about the case?"

Logan sighed, rubbing his temples. "I get the feeling *you* know more than *I* do."

I waved a hand. "Do you know how the curator died? I mean, it *could* have been a heart attack, right? Mystery solved." I said it half-seriously, quoting Mr. Roberts' hopeful theory. It made Logan laugh for the first time that morning, but the sound was short-lived.

"I guess we need to talk to Arthur."

I nodded, ready to strategize, but Logan's glance at his watch froze us mid-plan.

"Oh boy. I have to go." He grabbed Bruno's leash, then hesitated and handed it back to me. "Dana's lawyer is coming. I

Art, Vendors and Forgery

promised I'd be there. See you this afternoon? Evening? Later?"

I opened my mouth, but he was already halfway up the path.

"Great, Bruno," I muttered, watching him disappear. "They show up, mess up our day, and vanish."

Bruno wagged his tail like this whole thing was a great adventure.

"You're right," I sighed. "Let's go back to the office. At least *Linda* will appreciate our presence."

Chapter 15

The Mayor had been right about Linda. She was not happy that morning—but her face lit up the moment she saw me walk into the office.

"Thank goodness, Margaret. It's been a crazy morning," she said, hurrying out from behind her desk with a stack of papers in hand, a pen tucked behind her ear, and her readers perched on her forehead. "The playground inspection approvals are due today, the invoices for the new senior equipment need authorizing, and the art festival vendors are still waiting on you to check their permits. We have to assign them a location in the park, and they keep calling about storage and supply deliveries I can't answer. Oh—and let's not forget the candlelight dinner planning."

Art, Vendors and Forgery

I sighed and took the papers from her. "We've got this, Linda. Do not—"

"Margaret!" Bert's voice bellowed from his office at the far end of the department. "We've got a problem!"

Linda let out a long, theatrical exhale. "It's not an emergency, Bert. I already told you what to do."

Bruno trotted to stand beside us, and Bert gave him an enthusiastic scratch. I opened my mouth to remind Bert that Bruno was technically on duty—his vest said as much—but I didn't get the chance.

"Look, boss, I get that we deal with these vendors every year," Bert said, gesturing emphatically. "And I know they all want reassurance. But with no chief and another break-in at the Community Center—"

"Another break-in?" I interrupted.

Bert shook his head, waving it off. "No, no. I mean the Hudson thing. That just happened a few weeks ago, and people remember that kind of stuff."

Linda crossed her arms. "Bert, for the last time, you don't need to explain things to the vendors. Just tell them the city's coordinating with the police, and the park has a security system."

"Easy for you to say," Bert muttered. "No one's screaming in *your* ear, threatening to pull out of the festival."

I raised both hands before things escalated. "Okay, listen. Bert—next time someone asks about safety, tell them the Mayor's naming a new pro-term chief tonight, and that we're already coordinating with the department to ensure festival security. Do *not* mention the Community Center. If they ask, say you have no information."

Bert scratched the back of his head, then gave a slow nod and a smile. "Got it."

I turned back to Linda, but—

"What about the museum?" Bert piped up again.

This time, my curiosity—and caution—kicked in. "What about the museum?"

"They've been calling nonstop, asking about the safety of the pieces they sent to us."

"The pieces? Did we get any art pieces?" I turned to Linda, who looked just as confused.

"Who's been calling?" I asked. "When?"

Bert flipped open his notebook, thumbing through a few spiral-bound pages. "The first call came the day before yesterday, in the afternoon. A guy named Darts—no, maybe Derts?

Hard to tell. He had a thick accent. He was asking for someone named Rodriguez and got upset when I said I didn't know anyone by that name. Then he hung up. After that, a woman called asking about the authorization to release the art pieces—but I had no idea what she was talking about either."

I blinked, trying to wrap my head around what I was hearing. "Wait. Did you say Rodriguez?"

Bert nodded slowly.

"That's not a person—that's the painting. *The* painting. The one by Sebastián Rodriguez that's been in the museum since I can remember."

Bert looked blank. Not surprising. I made a mental note to support Mrs. Roberts' crusade to get local art more recognition.

"And the woman—did she give her name?"

He shook his head. "Sorry, boss. She was just really mad. Said we didn't have the proper authorization and threatened to call the Mayor."

"I doubt the Mayor answered *any* calls since Chief Anderson left," Linda muttered. "He's too busy trying to figure out the police situation. I bet he's more concerned with the meeting tonight than whatever else is happening in the city."

I couldn't disagree. Not out loud, anyway.

I took the paperwork from Linda and retreated into my office. But as I shuffled through the stack, my mind wasn't on playgrounds or senior equipment. It was on those calls Bert got.

If the curator had already been asking about the painting, that meant he *knew* it wasn't there. So why would he be at the museum—*at night*? And who was the woman? Could it have been Dana? She might need authorization to release pieces. Or could it have been Mrs. Roberts, pretending to be someone else, trying to track the painting's location?

The more I thought about it, the more I found myself wishing—*really* wishing—that Mr. Durst had died of a heart attack after all.

"Can I bother you for a moment?" Sophie asked, peeking from the doorframe.

I smiled and moved the last few folders on my desk aside. "Not bothering me at all. What's up?"

Art, Vendors and Forgery

She stepped inside carefully, as if afraid to make noise—funny, considering she was already so quiet. Sophie had always reminded me of a shadow with glasses: small, soft-spoken, and somehow always unnoticed. I probably looked the same when I first started my internship all those years ago, drowning in my mom's oversized blazer.

"We finished checking the storage room," she said, holding up a tablet. "Everything is still there, but I made a spreadsheet to help organize the inventory by category and date. I think Mrs. Oak liked it."

I took the tablet from her and scrolled through the spreadsheet. It was impressively detailed—categories, descriptions, purchase dates, costs, even notes about where each item had been used before.

"I'm sure Linda loved this. It's going to make her life so much easier. Great job, Sophie."

Her cheeks flushed, but she stood up a little straighter, clearly proud.

"I really appreciate you coming in. We've got a busy few weeks ahead, and the break-in threw a wrench into everything. I'm sure Martin is missing you on the first floor."

She gave me a shy smile and turned to leave,

but paused just before reaching the door. Taking a deep breath, she stepped back in.

"I was wondering..." She cleared her throat. "The festival used to have a kids' arts and crafts table, right? I didn't see it on the current list."

I nodded with a sigh. "I know. I loved that table when I was a kid—and I was hoping to take Darcy this year. But the truth is, we just don't have enough staff to run the program."

Her shoulders dropped along with her voice. "Got it. I understand. There's just so much going on."

"What are you working on now?" I asked.

She tucked her hair behind her ear and glanced at her tablet. "Norman and I are organizing the candlelight dinner. Terry's handling the bake-off and the culinary stands, but he said he couldn't take on anything else."

I chuckled. "Of course Terry's handling the food."

"He was thrilled when I said we'd take care of the rest."

"How excited are you about dinner planning?"

She hesitated, forcing a polite smile. "It's fine. I like organizing things. It should be okay to finalize the timeline and setup."

"How about you let Norman and me take

the dinner off your plate, and you help me with something else instead?"

Her eyes lit up, and I could see her trying not to look too eager. That confirmed my hunch.

"What do you think about coordinating the kids' art tables? It's the one part of the festival that's really been bothering me. Without a Rec Programs Director, I didn't think we could pull it off."

Sophie's eyes widened. "I—I don't know if I can do that. I've never worked on anything like it before."

I picked up my phone and called for Linda. "I just saw how organized you are—this spreadsheet is the hardest part of running a program like that. I think you'd be great at it."

Linda appeared at the door, half-curious, half-worried. "Yes?"

"I just asked Sophie to coordinate the kids' art program. What do you think?"

"Yes! That would be *great!*" Linda said without missing a beat.

Sophie smiled, though I could tell she was still nervous. "But what if I can't get it done in time?"

I waved her concern away. "We're not advertising it, so there's no public expectation.

Just set it up outside the main layout. If it comes together, wonderful. If not, we haven't lost anything."

She giggled and nodded. "Okay. I'll do it."

"Awesome! There should be a file with past festival plans. You can use it as a reference, but feel free to bring in your own ideas."

"What about supplies?" she asked. "Should I buy more or try to use what's in the storage room?"

I turned to Linda. "Do you know if Sophie can use anything from storage?"

"What stuff?" Linda asked. "There might be a couple of kids' art stands left over, but I'm not sure what else is there."

Sophie held up her tablet again and showed Linda the spreadsheet. After scrolling through for a few seconds, Linda nodded slowly.

"I don't remember ordering some of this paint... I'm sure it was Tara who did it."

She looked down and sighed. The mention of Tara's name hit a nerve for both of us. It was still hard to believe she'd been involved in Councilmember Hudson's murder. They'd been coworkers. Friends.

"In that case," I said, "feel free to use what we have. Let us know if you need anything else, okay?"

Art, Vendors and Forgery

Both women left my office a moment later, but I didn't go back to my paperwork. I stared at the tablet Sophie left behind, and a chill crept up my spine. Something about those supplies... they felt like more than just leftover paint and craft sticks.

Chapter 16

Logan called just before the end of the day and asked if we could meet at my mom's house. He sounded more like himself again, so I hoped he had good news—or at least some kind of news.

What I didn't expect was to find him sitting on the porch with Darcy, holding a wildly colorful ice cream cone in his hand.

The moment I opened the door, Bruno shot out of the car like a rocket and didn't stop until he reached Darcy. And by "greeted her," I mean he knocked her flat onto her back, licked her face like it was made of peanut butter... and promptly devoured her ice cream.

"Bruno!" I shouted.

He ignored me completely—though, to be fair, Darcy's laughter was loud enough to

Art, Vendors and Forgery

drown me out. Maybe he hadn't heard me. Maybe.

From his spot on the steps, Logan smiled and shook his head. He offered his own ice cream cone to Bruno, who gave it a quick sniff, then trotted right back to Darcy, more interested in play than food.

"I guess rainbow swirl isn't his flavor," I said.

"You don't say," Logan replied with a grin.

Darcy peeked her head out from behind Bruno. "But *you* liked it, right?"

It was genuinely amusing how quickly Logan's face lit up under her hopeful stare. He took a dramatic bite, then nodded enthusiastically, maybe too enthusiastically.

"Hey, girl," Logan said to her. "Think I can borrow your mom for a couple hours? I need help with some work."

Darcy gave him a suspicious look. "Do you mean an *investigation*?"

Logan scratched the back of his head and mumbled something, but Darcy's giggles cut him off.

"She's the best at finding stuff! Whenever I lose my things, she *always* knows where they are. I can share her with you," she said with the authority of a judge, lifting a finger like my mom always did when she was about to issue a firm rule. "But she has to *eat*, okay? You better get her food. Promise?"

Logan stood up and gave her a serious salute. "Miss Willow, you have my word."

Darcy gave me a lightning-fast hug, called for Bruno, and dashed inside the house.

"Let's go," Logan said, already heading down the steps.

"Wait, what? Can I at least go in and change—"

"Nope. Sorry. We need to catch someone outside the station, and he moves fast."

"What? Who?" I asked, jogging after him as he opened the passenger door of his car.

"Arthur," he said. "We need to figure out the cause of death, Maggie."

I groaned and tossed my purse inside as I slid into the seat. Despite my dramatic sigh, curiosity was already sparking.

I just *really* hoped I wouldn't have to see any dead bodies.

I expected we'd head to the police station when Logan said we were going to catch Arthur after

Art, Vendors and Forgery

work. Maybe the back entrance, away from too many watchful eyes. What I *didn't* expect was to circle around the entire town square and park in a nearly empty lot behind the community center—the kind of place that felt too quiet for this time of day.

"He parks back here to get a walk in before work," Logan said as he cut the engine. "Says it clears his head."

"That's... oddly wholesome," I muttered. "But why not just tell him you wanted to talk?"

Logan drummed his fingers on the steering wheel and looked out the windshield. "Because he doesn't want to talk to me."

I frowned. Before I could ask, he added, "Maggie, he knows what I want. He just doesn't want to be the guy who breaks the rules."

A slight grin tugged at the corner of his mouth as he turned to me. "That's why you're here."

"Me?" I leaned back, startled. "Why me?"

He chuckled, low and knowing. "Of course you don't know. Maggie, he's had a crush on you since high school. That's why he always volunteered to be your lab partner and hung around your place."

I burst out laughing. "He didn't have a

crush on me, Logan. It was *Lucy*. She was always at my house, remember? *That's* why he was there."

Logan frowned, rubbing a hand down his face like I'd just cracked a cherished childhood belief. "You sure? He never said anything."

I crossed my arms and raised a brow. "Really? How exactly would that conversation have gone? 'Hey Logan, while you were quarterbacking and pitching games, I was pining over your girlfriend'?"

He leaned toward me in the cramped space of the car, and somehow that little shift felt too close.

"So you *did* think I was a handsome sports star," he said, teasing.

I rolled my eyes and turned to the window, hoping he couldn't hear the uptick in my heartbeat. "I didn't say—I think someone's coming," I said, spotting a figure walking briskly across the path that connected the lot to the back of City Hall.

"There's Arthur," I added.

Logan had already opened the door. "Perfect timing. Let's go."

He didn't wait for me. He jogged toward the man, waving. "Arthur!"

Arthur jumped and let out a sharp yelp,

Art, Vendors and Forgery

stumbling off the path. "For the love of—Logan, are you trying to give me a heart attack?"

Bent over, hands on his knees, he looked winded and flushed.

"I tried to catch you this morning," Logan said. "You dodged me."

"I *was* busy," Arthur snapped, straightening. "And I *still* can't talk to you."

Logan crossed his arms. "But you talked to Maggie a few weeks ago. About *my* case."

Arthur's eyes flicked toward me as if only now realizing I'd followed them. "Hi, Maggie," he said politely. Then, turning back to Logan: "That was different. She didn't know... it was just different."

"Oh sure," Logan said, with a grin. "She's prettier than me, right?"

Arthur's cheeks flushed as he flailed for an appropriate answer. "I mean, she is, but that wasn't why—"

"Logan," I said, cutting him off. "Arthur was just trying to help. You know that. And he put his job on the line to do it—*because* you were railroading my brother-in-law."

Logan opened his mouth, but Arthur raised a hand.

"I'm sorry, Maggie," he said. His voice had dropped lower, heavier. "Your mom must be devastated. I was shocked when Warren went ahead and arrested all of them. Honestly, I don't think he has enough. But... he thinks he does. If Chief Anderson were still around, this never would've happened."

I stepped forward, lowering my voice. "So... you think Ben's innocent?"

Arthur exhaled and rubbed the back of his neck. "I like Morales. And because I *know* him, I question everything. But the evidence seems solid. It's strong enough that I—wait, Maggie."

I blinked at him. "What? I didn't *do* anything."

"You're doing it again."

I raised my brows innocently. "Doing what?"

"You're making me talk about the case! And neither you nor Logan should be—"

"But you just said it," I cut in. "Warren's not looking for the truth. He's building a case. I can't let Ben take the fall just because Warren's trying to settle some old grudge."

Arthur's features shifted. The anger melted, just a little, into something like guilt. After a beat, he sighed.

"How can I help?"

Before I could answer, Logan clapped his

friend on the back. But Arthur held up a finger.

"I hope you *really* understand what you're doing here, Logan."

"I do," Logan said, his tone shifting—deeper, more serious. "This could cost us everything. Our jobs. Our reputations. Maybe worse."

Arthur rubbed his temples. "No. You're not risking your job. You're giving Maggie a pass into every future investigation. And mine. You *can't* take that back once it starts."

Logan blinked. "That's not what I'm—"

"Don't be naive," Arthur snapped. He jabbed a finger at me. "Once you open that door, how are you going to deny her access later? You're setting a precedent."

Logan turned to me.

I just smiled and lifted my shoulders.

Logan groaned. "She's already doing it."

Chapter 17

Although I wasn't sure I wanted to hear about the murder while eating, I couldn't deny I was starving—and the tavern was a solid idea.

"Did you get the lab results back?" Logan asked Arthur after we'd ordered.

Arthur shook his head, his expression tight. "Might take another two days. I had to request an extended toxicology panel."

"So... it wasn't a heart attack?" I asked, already knowing how naïve it sounded. The last shred of hope that this had all been some tragic accident vanished like smoke.

Logan reached across the table and gave my hand a squeeze. It helped—briefly. Until I remembered he wasn't only worried for Ben. Dana—his ex-wife—was tangled in all this

Art, Vendors and Forgery

too. And I still didn't know what to make of *that*.

"Extended tox screen?" Logan repeated. "You're thinking poison?"

"Definitely," Arthur said grimly. "He hit the ground hard—blunt force to the back of the head might've been fatal on its own—but the burns inside..." He stopped, suddenly aware of me. "Sorry."

I wanted to tell him it was fine. That I could handle it. But that would've been a lie—and one I'd likely pay for in nightmares. Instead, I offered a polite out.

"I can step away if this is... sensitive."

"Not important," Logan said quickly. "We'll stick to the general picture."

Arthur nodded and took a sip of his drink. "The presence of toxins was clear."

"Toxins?" Logan asked. "As in plural?"

"Yes. Traces of several substances, all pointing toward poisoning. I just don't know what kind. The effects overlap when the dosage is high enough. I'm starting with a heavy metals panel."

"That's awful." My mind jumped to Troy's murders only a few weeks ago. "Does that mean the killer knew him? Hated him enough to make it personal?"

"Could be," Arthur said, but before he could continue, the waitress arrived with our food.

I stared at my plate longer than I meant to. Apparently long enough for both men to notice.

"I don't think anyone hates *you*, Maggie," Logan said gently. "And I'm sure it is delicious."

"Plus, the guy had no taste buds anyway," Arthur added, reaching for his fork.

My curiosity perked. "You mean... he had terrible taste? Or—?"

"No, officially. He had ageusia. Complete loss of taste—been that way for about ten years."

"You got that from the autopsy?"

Arthur chuckled. "No. Medical records. The guy was a walking collection of ailments—diabetes, recurring infections, chronic vitamin deficiencies, mild depression. You name it."

"So I was right," I said, glancing at Logan. "Whoever poisoned him had to know his medical history. Or at least, know him well enough to exploit it."

Logan rubbed his jaw. "Which means it couldn't have been Ben or Dana. They barely

Art, Vendors and Forgery

knew the guy. But Mrs. Roberts... you said she knew him, right?"

I didn't like how easily suspicion fell on her. Again. But I nodded. "She mentioned they'd met."

I didn't get a chance to elaborate.

Arthur's posture changed suddenly. He pushed his food aside, his expression darkening.

"You don't know, do you, Logan?"

My stomach clenched. Whatever Arthur was about to say, I had a feeling it would change everything.

"What don't I know?" Logan asked, voice sharpening. "Spit it out."

Arthur cleared his throat, reluctant. "Tricia told me they found evidence connecting Dana and the victim—Scott Durst—in a personal relationship."

Logan went still. Not just motionless —*frozen*. For a moment I thought he hadn't heard. Then he shook his head and gave a hollow laugh.

"She works at the museum. He's a curator. Of course they knew each other. It's professional. That doesn't mean—"

"Sorry, Logan," Arthur cut in. "The evidence shows a *personal* relationship. And not a recent one. Tricia said it spanned at least two years. Maybe longer."

Logan sat back, stunned. Then leaned forward again, arms crossed, jaw tight.

"No. That's not possible. He lives in the city. Dana hates long-distance relationships—I know that. And he's what, ten years older?"

"Eight," Arthur said softly. It may as well have been a shout.

"Sorry, man. I know this hits hard. I wish it hadn't been me who—"

Logan waved him off, shaking his head slowly. I half expected him to slam the table, raise his voice—*something*. But he just sat there, his confusion etched across his face, the pain leaking through despite his best effort to contain it.

"What about Ben?" he asked, clearly trying to steer the conversation elsewhere.

"Right. Ben," Arthur said. "Dana called him that morning."

That stopped me. I had no idea why Dana would've called Ben. But then again, I'd never hidden my feelings about her, especially not at home. If Ben knew her, it wasn't something he would've shared with *me*.

"That can't be all," Logan said. "She probably called several people."

Art, Vendors and Forgery

Arthur hesitated. Then turned to me.

That look he'd given Logan earlier—that cautious, *this-is-gonna-hurt* expression—was now pointed directly at me.

"Warren found a photograph of your mom, Maggie."

My blood turned cold. "A *what*?"

My voice came out louder than I meant. A few heads turned, but no one seemed to really register the outburst.

"Is he trying to frame my mom, too?" I asked.

"No!" Arthur said quickly. "No, nothing like that. But... the picture had a dedication on the back. Addressed to Ben. He admitted it was his. And he confessed to being at the museum the day of the murder."

My pulse roared in my ears. Ben... at the museum? That day?

I knew in my bones Ben didn't kill anyone. Especially not like this. But even I could see how bad this looked. No alibi. A secret visit. Dana's name in the mix.

Suddenly, none of us were interested in our food anymore.

Montie Red

Logan drove me home in a heavy, almost comforting silence. I was grateful for it. I didn't know what to say, and my thoughts were spinning too fast to make room for conversation.

I hadn't mentioned what Mr. Roberts said about finding the painting in Dana's office. Arthur hadn't brought it up either, which made me wonder—was Mr. Roberts lying? Or did he have deeper connections than I'd realized? I wanted to tell Logan, but now didn't feel like the right time. Not after everything he'd just learned about Dana and Durst. I didn't want to add fuel to an already painful fire—not unless I was sure it was true.

As for Ben... I didn't know what to think. I wanted to ask him what he was doing at the museum, or why Dana had called him that morning. But of the three people caught up in this mess, Ben was the only one still behind bars. Not that surprising, considering he used to be the police chief.

When Logan parked in front of my house, he finally spoke.

"We'll figure it out, Maggie," he said gently. "I need to talk to Dana, clear a few things up—but I think it's better if I do that alone."

"Of course." I reached for the door handle but didn't open it right away.

Art, Vendors and Forgery

He noticed. "What is it?" he asked, his voice light and teasing—which somehow made what I had to say even harder.

I turned toward him and took a steadying breath. "Dana... do you really think she'll tell you the truth?"

He groaned, glancing away. "I know you don't like her, but she's not a bad person. I know her."

"Do you?" I asked, gently but firmly. "You looked surprised—really surprised—when Arthur told you she'd had an affair with Durst—"

"No," he cut me off, and the look in his eyes was sharp. "You're right. You don't know the history between us, and honestly, it's not part of this case. She didn't kill him. Just like you're certain Ben's innocent, I know Dana is too."

I nodded and finally opened the door, but before stepping out, I said what I'd been holding back for days.

"I didn't even know you married her, Logan."

He blinked, then let out a dry laugh. "Well, Maggie, it's not like we exchange wedding invitations."

"Right," I said softly, climbing out of the

Montie Red

car. I shut the door gently, careful not to slam it, and walked toward the house—calmly, even though I wanted to stomp the whole way there.

If I'd ever gotten married, maybe I *would've* invited him. But this only confirmed what I'd feared for a long time: we weren't really friends. Maybe we never had been.

"Hi, Maggie," my mom called, sitting on the front step. "Will you have some tea with me?"

Chapter 18

I let my mom sit at the kitchen counter while I filled the kettle and set it to boil. It was easy to see how the last couple of days had worn her down. Her eyes were puffy, and her shoulders drooped like she was carrying the weight of the world.

"Darcy told me you were having dinner with Logan?" she asked.

I frowned and shook my head. "Not exactly. He wanted me to help him talk to Arthur."

She nodded, eyes lingering on the fruit basket beside her. "I suppose he can't officially be on the case because of Dana?"

The kettle whistled—perfect timing. I turned away to grab the mugs, grateful for the excuse to avoid looking at her while I gathered my thoughts.

"Yeah, he's not happy about it. He thought Arthur might open up more if I was there." I chuckled, remembering what Logan had said. "He thinks Arthur had a crush on me in high school."

My mom let out a soft laugh, though it was tinged with sadness. When I turned back to hand her a cup, she looked more concerned than amused.

"Mom, what is it? Did you talk to Ben?"

She shook her head, taking a deep breath. "I'm not part of his family…"

I swore silently and sat down beside her. "I can talk to Andrew. Maybe he still knows that lawyer—"

"Ben doesn't want my help," she interrupted, her voice steadier now. "Tricia told me he talked to one of those court-appointed lawyers you get when you can't afford one. She's worried, and that tells me how bad this is getting. Maggie, I'm scared he'll end up in prison. And you know what happens to cops in those places."

The thought made me shudder. I reached for her hand. "Let's not go there. We'll find out who this lawyer is and talk to him—"

Art, Vendors and Forgery

"Maggie," she gripped my hand, her voice firm but pleading. "I wouldn't ask if I had another option. And believe me, I hate asking this of you. I don't want you in danger. But I just don't trust anyone at that station anymore. Did you know Ben fired our deputy years ago? Tricia told me. And now that same deputy could have influence over this case. She's worried about whether Ben will get a fair trial. And Logan can't help."

Her voice cracked, and she paused to breathe. I used the moment to squeeze her hand.

"We'll figure this out. I know it looks bad, but something isn't adding up."

My mom gave a weak chuckle and patted my hand. "This is the first time I'm glad you didn't listen to me."

I bit my lip and hid behind my mug, taking a sip of tea. Before I could say anything else, my phone lit up with a text from Sandie.

You home?

Yes. I replied.

On my way.

"I don't think Logan was so wrong about Arthur," Mom said. When I looked up, there was a mischievous twinkle in her eye. "I'm sure he liked Lucy—but I don't think it was just her he had a crush on."

I groaned and shook my head—right as the front door burst open.

"I'm so glad you two are up!" Sandie announced dramatically.

"Shhh!" Mom and I both hushed her, and I pointed toward the ceiling.

"If you don't want the other Willow girl to join us," my mom whispered, "you'd better lower your voice."

Sandie clapped a hand over her mouth and tiptoed her way into the kitchen.

"Did you watch the council meeting?" she asked.

My mom raised a brow. "Since when do you care about local politics?"

Sandie poured herself a cup of tea and slid onto a stool. "Since my husband came back from the community center with the juiciest gossip: the Mayor had *big* news!"

With everything I'd uncovered today, I'd completely forgotten about the Mayor's announcement.

"The Mayor named Detective Logan Forest the new interim Chief of Police while Anderson's on leave!"

Art, Vendors and Forgery

My mom turned to me, wide-eyed, but before I could say a word, Sandie gasped.

"Wait—did you know? Of course you did!"

"This is good, right?" my mom asked hopefully.

I lifted my shoulders in a small shrug. "Did the Mayor mention me?"

Sandie frowned. "Why would he? You're not part of the police department."

I let out a breath, relieved I wasn't publicly tied to the case. But the news stirred a new unease in me. How was this going to sit with Deputy Warren—and what would it mean for Ben?

"I was with the Mayor when Anderson announced his departure," I said.

"You what?" Sandie blurted.

"Shhh!" my mom warned again, swatting the air between them.

"It wasn't planned," I clarified. "I was there for another reason. But that's not the point. Logan was involved when Ben fired Warren. What do you think Warren's going to feel about Logan being promoted over him? I mean, by rank, the deputy should've been next in line."

My mom slapped the table and gasped. "Oh boy! Do you think that's why Dana's involved in this mess? Just like with Ben—maybe this Deputy Warren is framing them?"

It felt good to talk openly about the case with my mom and Sandie. I guessed three heads thought better than one, and with them, I didn't need to keep anything back. They were both on Ben's side and agreed with me that Dana's behavior was suspicious. I wasn't saying she did it—I truly didn't believe that—but there was definitely something she was hiding, beyond the painting in her office.

"That poor guy," Sandie said. "Imagine how terrible it must be to live without knowing how things taste!"

I nodded in agreement, and my next sip of tea had a glorious flavor.

"But wouldn't you think that concoction had a strong smell?" my mom asked. "I understand whoever gave it to him must've been close, but still... or maybe he couldn't smell either?"

I shook my head, understanding her point.

"I don't think that would've mattered," Sandie said, with a level of confidence that

Art, Vendors and Forgery

made me brace for a joke. "Think about it. The guy worked with old paintings. As a curator, he had to restore a lot of them and their frames. Do you know how strong those solvents are?"

My mom smiled at her. "Of course, Sandie. But you wouldn't drink those, and that's why I always made you open your window when you were painting."

"Sure, but your hands end up reeking no matter what. Sometimes, even after you wash them."

"Your hands didn't smell like paint, Sandie," my mom said. "I would've made you wash them again!"

Sandie shook her head and looked straight at me. "That may be true, but the smell stays in your head. If you're around it all day, every day, those solvents—which are probably way stronger than my regular oils and acrylics—can mess with your brain. So even if that concoction smelled like pure gasoline, he might not have even noticed. Just saying."

I finished my tea, still thinking about Sandie's theory. Scott Durst must've been around paint and solvents constantly—maybe even sculpting materials, which could be toxic too.

"That does make some sense," my mom

admitted. "But getting back to the important part—Ben. I doubt he even knew this curator. Ben knows nothing about art. How is Warren blaming him?"

My heart sank, and I could swear the room's temperature dropped. My mom didn't miss my reaction. She took a breath and asked softly:

"Maggie... do you know something?"

"I—Arthur said—kind of, but I don't think it's..." I sighed, gathering my thoughts. "Arthur said the police found a photo of you in the museum. A dedicated one."

"Of Mom?" Sandie dropped her hands onto the counter, missing her cup by a hair. "How?"

My mom's gaze dropped to the table. I reached out and took her hand.

"Just because he had it doesn't mean he killed Durst."

"I know," she whispered. "I just don't know what to think. We had such a lovely conversation when he dropped off Darcy... and apparently, he kept my photo all these years. But he doesn't want my help?"

I smiled gently. "That's easy, Mom. Why didn't *you* want *me* involved in this case? Or

Art, Vendors and Forgery

the council member's murder a few weeks ago?"

Sandie wrapped her arms around my mom's shoulders and rested her head against hers. "He loves you, Mom. We'll clear his name so you can kill him later."

We all laughed, the sound helping clear the heaviness from the air. When my mom spoke again, she sounded almost back to normal.

"All right, so I understand why Warren arrested Ben. But what about Mrs. Roberts and Dana?"

"Well, Mrs. Roberts is a little murky," I said. "She was obsessed with having the Rodriguez painting included in the festival. She pressured both the Mayor and the museum's director, DeVoir, to allow it. That's why it was being evaluated. And she's supposedly the one who received the fake Historical Preservation's email saying DeVoir was taking the painting that night instead of waiting for our scheduled meeting."

Sandie crossed her arms and sat back down. "That's suspicious. Did you see the email?"

I shook my head. "Mr. Roberts said the police took all their devices, and they didn't want to make things worse by logging into her account."

I rested my hands on the counter. "She also owns a strange replica of the Rodriguez. I'm no expert, but to me, it looks better than the one I remember in the museum."

"Maybe you *need* an expert," Sandie said casually, brushing away imaginary crumbs.

I opened my mouth, but my mom cut in.

"No! Sandie, you're about to have a baby and helping your friend with her wedding. One of my girls involved in this is enough."

We both nodded, but I was sure the idea stuck in all our heads. After all, Sandie had studied art in college before she dropped out.

"What about Dana?" Mom asked, clearly changing the subject.

I sighed and felt myself sinking into my chair. "Apparently, Dana had a relationship with Durst... and she called Ben that afternoon." I kept Mr. Roberts' information to myself—not because I didn't trust them, but because I needed to verify it first.

My mom shook her head and closed her eyes.

"Do you know why she would've called Ben?" I asked, concerned by her reaction.

"No," she whispered. "I thought he disliked that girl as much as you do."

Art, Vendors and Forgery

I tried to keep a straight face, but Sandie didn't let me off the hook.

"Oh, come on, Maggie. You *hate* Dana. Probably for good reason."

I ignored that and pressed on. "Why doesn't Ben like her?"

It was my mom who answered. "When Logan joined the force, Ben took him under his wing. It was sweet, actually. He even let Logan live in his apartment when his marriage fell apart. Ben didn't appreciate what Dana did to that poor boy."

She pointed a finger at me and Sandie. "And no—I'm not saying another word. This is Logan's life, and I won't gossip about it."

I frowned at the irony, considering how much of *my* life she freely shared with the entire town, but I didn't argue. Mostly because I wasn't sure I wanted to know.

Chapter 19

The next morning, I walked into the police station with Bruno trotting faithfully by my side. I wasn't sure I actually wanted to see Logan—but when Tricia told me he wasn't in and that he'd asked me to keep Bruno, disappointment hit harder than I expected.

I almost asked where he was or if I should come back later, but held my tongue. His new position as Chief had been announced the night before, and I figured it came with more responsibilities—and less time for dogs, or me.

"Maggie! Really?" Norman called the second I stepped off the elevator.

"Really?" I echoed, not sure what I was defending yet.

Art, Vendors and Forgery

He rolled his eyes. "The candlelight dinner? You want me to plan a *fancy* dinner?"

"It's just a community event, Norman. A little gathering. I'm sure we can figure it out."

"We?" he asked, eyebrow arched. "Are you working on it too?"

I gave him my most innocent smile, but Linda's sharp look said she was not in the mood for nonsense.

"Come on, Margaret," Norman groaned. "How am I supposed to plan this? It sounds like a wedding. And I did *not* do well on that one."

Linda crossed her arms with the gravity of a judge delivering a sentence. "Well, you'd better learn fast, because there's no pre-made plan for this one. We've never done a candlelight dinner before. And with the chance of rain..."

"Rain?" Norman blinked. "I didn't even consider that!"

Bruno sat down next to him and gave his leg a sympathetic nudge.

"It'll be okay, Norman," I said. "It's easier than a wedding. No dresses, no invitations, no gift registry."

Linda snorted. "Sure. But we *do* need tables and chairs. Then there's the food—warming stations, cleaning crews. And don't even get me started on flowers, wine, and a backup location in case of weather 'altercations.'"

Norman paled. His hands twitched. "I can't do this alone. It's going to be a disaster."

I placed a hand on his shoulder, speaking slowly. "Listen, Norman. Talk to Terry. He's already got vendors lined up. They'll show off their culinary skills and handle the food and drinks. Linda can give you the number for Mrs. Gladis Williams—just look as panicked as you do now and she'll take care of flowers and decorations."

Norman blinked.

"As for tables," I continued, "ask Bert. We can borrow the ones from the salons at the community center or the Country Club."

Linda narrowed her eyes. "And what about the rain?"

I took a step back and lifted my shoulders. "I'll get back to you on that one."

Norman laughed, a little too nervously, but the color was starting to return to his face. He still didn't move until Linda gave him a sharp look and pointed toward Terry's desk.

Art, Vendors and Forgery

My desk still held the same tower of folders from earlier, and I had no desire to sit and read through contracts. But when Linda knocked on my door and walked in with Deputy Warren, suddenly, all that paperwork looked a lot more appealing.

"Deputy Warren," I exclaimed—just as I managed to bump the entire stack of papers straight into him.

He caught most of them, while Linda knelt to help gather the rest.

"I'm so sorry," I said, flustered. "I wasn't expecting to see anyone and... sorry again."

To my surprise, he smiled. A real, genuine, understanding smile. It caught me off guard—especially after everything I'd heard about him, and his coldness, both on the night of the murder and earlier, when I saw him talking with Logan.

"Are you going to arrest her?" Linda asked, her tone more serious than I expected as she stacked the fallen folders on my desk.

"For attacking me with a bunch of folders?" He shook his head, still smiling. "No. Absolutely not."

I chuckled at that, mostly at Linda's truly perplexed expression.

"What can I do for you, Deputy?" I asked, straightening the edges of the papers.

Linda lingered by the door, clearly stalling to hear his answer. If Warren noticed, he didn't comment. He simply said, "I was hoping to ask you a few more questions about the murder of Mr. Durst."

I gestured toward the chair across from my desk and waited until Linda had finally, reluctantly left before continuing. Warren sat down. Bruno padded over to greet him.

"Morning, Officer Bruno," Warren said, giving him a good scratch behind the ears. "I hear you've been helping out with his training."

I started to reply, but he held up a hand.

"That wasn't a question. And by the way, I'm impressed. This guy used to be... how can I put it? A very active spirit in the canine world."

Bruno had already settled at his feet, panting contentedly, clearly soaking up the praise.

"He *is* a special spirit," I said, smiling. "My mom and daughter have had a lot to do with that. I'm sure of it."

Warren nodded, and for a moment his expression shifted—uncertainty? Thoughtfulness? I wasn't sure. So I waited for the questions to come.

"Well," he said, sitting up straighter, "I better start before Linda storms in and pulls me out. I hear Mrs. Oak doesn't take kindly to people wasting your time."

"Linda's someone to fear when she's angry," I said lightly. The second it left my mouth, I regretted it. Way to throw your best assistant under the bus.

But Warren actually chuckled. "I know. We play on opposite pickleball teams."

A wave of relief passed through me. I was starting to feel more curious about him now—not just suspicious.

"I won't take up much of your time," he continued, switching to a more formal tone. "I wanted to ask about Mrs. Roberts' involvement in the art festival. Specifically, her interest in having a high-value painting out of the museum that weekend."

It wasn't an easy question, mostly because I didn't know the answer myself. So I went with the truth.

"I'm not completely sure, Deputy. This is my first festival."

He nodded, like he already knew that. "All right. Then how would you describe Mrs.

Roberts' participation in the planning? Is she helpful? Difficult? Obsessive—especially when it comes to the painting?"

"I wouldn't say obsessive," I said. "But she's passionate. She really wants the piece to be more accessible to the people of Apple Creek."

He raised an eyebrow. "Is the museum not accessible?" Then, quickly, he lifted his hands in apology. "Sorry, I'm not saying the idea is wrong. I love Apple Creek, and the festival is one of my favorites. I just question the wisdom of moving such an important piece without proper security."

He had a point. The mayor, Director DeVoir, and I had come to a similar conclusion. The painting was still under debate, and honestly, it should've been a hard no from the start.

"It's a big assumption," I admitted. "But the museum isn't always the most family-friendly place. The idea is that showcasing this piece in a public park could inspire kids. Help them believe in their own creativity."

He nodded slowly. "A noble cause. I'm still not sure I agree with the risk—but it's something."

He stood and walked toward the door.

Art, Vendors and Forgery

"Thank you for your time, Miss Willow. I hope I didn't interrupt your day too much."

"Not at all, Deputy," I said.

He smiled again, gave Bruno one last affectionate pat, and left.

I sat back in my chair, unsure what to make of that visit.

"What do you think, Bruno?" I asked, kneeling beside him to rub his ears. "If you and Chief Anderson liked him, maybe he's not so bad. Do you think he's just trying to do his job —not trying to blame Ben? Like Logan with Paul, maybe he didn't have a choice."

Bruno gave a soft, thoughtful *woof*.

"We need to figure this out, Bruno," I whispered. "Before someone else gets hurt."

Chapter 20

The morning flew by in a blur of paperwork. I had barely made a dent in the reports I'd been avoiding, and now I was supposed to start planning for fall events—while also staying ahead on winter ones. The strange thing about working in parks was how seasons overlapped. In the middle of July, I was booking pumpkin carving vendors and sending budget notes about artificial snow machines.

And speaking of the budget—probably my least favorite word in the English language—it sat on my desk like a fat toad, untouched.

"Margaret?" Linda peeked into my office.

I looked up from a spreadsheet that was giving me a headache.

Art, Vendors and Forgery

"Paul just called," she said. "He wants to know if you can meet him at the park."

Part of me was thrilled for an excuse to leave the office. Another part tensed. Paul didn't usually ask for meetings unless something was broken, leaking, or on fire.

"Did he sound worried or happy?"

Linda chuckled as she turned back to her desk. "He sounded annoyed you didn't answer your cell."

I checked my desk, then my purse. "Ugh. Left it in the car. Thanks, Linda!"

Grabbing my bag and Bruno's leash, I gave my dog a grin. "Let's go get some sun, buddy."

Before heading out, I popped my head back toward Linda's desk. "Want me to bring something for lunch?"

She waved me off with a dramatic sigh. "You may not be back until dinner. Or tomorrow morning. Bring snacks instead."

I laughed, but a twinge of guilt twisted in my stomach. She wasn't wrong. Every outing lately seemed to spin off into a new clue or complication.

I was halfway across the lobby when I saw Logan walking in from the parking lot. As a detective, he rarely wore a uniform—and I couldn't remember the last time I'd seen him in

175

one. Of course, he looked good. *Too* good. The ridiculous butterflies in my stomach stirred to life. But as he got closer, the look on his face clipped their wings and set my nerves on edge.

Bruno gave a soft bark and pulled slightly toward him.

"Hey, Bruno." Logan crouched down and scratched behind his ears. "I missed you. How was your morning?"

I doubted Bruno had any thoughts on budget spreadsheets, so I answered for him. "Uneventful. A sunbeam through the window was the highlight."

Logan smiled as he stood, but the expression faded quickly. "Sorry. I had to leave early. Didn't think Bruno needed to sit through a council meeting."

"That's right. Should I start calling you Chief Forest now?"

His jaw tightened. "Please don't. It's the last thing I need right now."

I blinked. "You don't want the job?"

"No. I never did." His voice dropped, rough and low. "I respected Chief Anderson. And Morales. But I never wanted *their* job."

I opened my mouth, then closed it again. After last night's conversation, I wasn't sure where we stood. I wasn't even sure if he was mad at me.

"Understood," I murmured. "I need to meet Paul at the park. Do you want Bruno back or—?"

"No." Logan pushed a hand through his hair and sighed. "Keep him with you today."

Then he paused and glanced toward the glass doors, like he was making sure we were still alone.

"Please be careful, Maggie."

That stopped me.

"I know you're not going to stop poking around," he continued quietly, "and I can't be as involved in this as I want to be. But if anything happens to you—"

He cut himself off and met my eyes. "Promise me you'll be careful. Please?"

My heart cracked open, just a little. The way he looked at me—like I was something fragile in a world full of sharp edges—was dangerous. It brought back the same flood of emotion I'd tried to ignore for years.

Before I could answer, the lobby door swung open.

"Chief Forest!" our eternally cheerful mayor called out, his voice bouncing off the walls. "We're late for our meeting with the city manager."

Logan groaned, which made me chuckle.

"You'd better go," I said. "He's not exactly the patient type."

He touched my arm lightly, stopping me again. His eyes locked on mine.

"Promise?"

I nodded. "I'll be careful. I promise."

He stood there for one more heartbeat—long enough to make my heart pound against my ribs—then turned and walked toward the mayor, leaving me breathless in the doorway.

Bruno pressed his nose to my hand.

"Come on, partner," I whispered. "Let's go see what Paul wants. And hope it doesn't involve another broken fountain or a body in the bushes."

"Do you ever answer your phone?" Sandie shouted the second I stepped into the park.

"What are you doing here?" I asked, only mildly surprised. After getting in my car earlier, I'd noticed ten missed calls from my sister, two from my mom, and one from Paul.

Art, Vendors and Forgery

I wasn't panicking—I'd already called Mom and confirmed she and Darcy were fine. Apparently, Sandie needed something for Lucy's wedding. Knowing my sister, though, I suspected that was just an excuse to dig into the murder. I was right.

"We need to talk to DeVoir," she declared like it was already decided. Before I could ask why, Paul approached.

"So, what do you think?" he said, hands on his hips, surveying his work.

I had to admit—it looked spectacular. The art festival I remembered was nothing like the little village Paul and his team had built in the park. The vendor stands, now assembled, were arranged like quaint streets leading to a central plaza. At the heart of it all stood the gazebo, reserved for the band and other events.

"This is amazing, Paul! I love it!" I exclaimed, wandering through the setup. The vendor booths were freshly painted and now resembled colorful little cottages.

He'd strung old-fashioned lightbulbs across the plaza, which I could already tell would be magical once lit at night. My favorite touch was the new yard tables and chairs—far more charming and communal than the usual park benches and picnic areas.

"We still need to connect the lights to city power," Paul said. "But that should be easy. Are you sure you want a big tent here?"

"A tent?" I frowned, picturing a giant white canopy ruining the charm of the art village.

"That's what Bert Smith told me," Paul replied, clearly not thrilled about the idea either. "Something about a dinner and the chance of rain?"

I rolled my eyes. "Forget the tent. And if Bert brings it up again, tell him I'll come up with a backup rain plan for the candlelight dinner."

"Candlelight dinner," Sandie repeated, looping her arm through Paul's and stepping closer. "That sounds romantic. Is this something new?"

I nodded, still admiring the space. Just two days ago, I would've bet the festival would be canceled. "It was Mrs. Roberts' idea."

"I love it," Sandie said, smiling up at Paul. "We should go."

Paul, caught in the spell of his weakness—my sister—sighed. He clearly wanted no part of a fancy dinner, but Sandie's giddy hug made it clear he'd already lost the battle.

"But you're not buying a new dress,

Art, Vendors and Forgery

Sandie," he added, shooting me a pleading look.

"Paul's right. No new dresses," I said, until I saw her pout. "But Paul will need a tuxedo."

Sandie clapped her hands. "Yes!"

"That's not happening," Paul grumbled.

"Fine, then a smoking jacket," I said. "Your choice."

He wisely chose to ignore that and switched topics. "Can you believe your sister's not here to admire my masterpiece? She's hunting you down instead. You should answer your phone more often, Margaret."

Sandie crossed her arms. "Exactly. You're distracting me, Maggie. We need to go to the museum. I've been thinking—what if Mrs. Roberts made up that email? We should ask DeVoir if he ever planned to send the painting out."

I opened my mouth to respond, but Bert interrupted.

"Margaret! Thank goodness you're here. We've got a few questions for you."

Sophie trailed behind him, looking far less confident. Bert marched over, clipboard in hand.

"I asked Harold to bring all the chairs and tables down from storage, but usually the catering company provides the tablecloths, chair covers, plates, and silverware."

"Terry can check with the country club and borrow those," I said. "I know they don't have an event that weekend, so it should work. He can call me if there's any issue."

Bert crossed his arms. "And are you going to answer the phone?"

I rolled my eyes as Sandie nodded her agreement.

"Hey! It's the first time I've missed calls, and you all survived."

"Fine," Bert muttered. "I'll talk to Terry. Sophie here found something interesting."

I turned my attention to her and noticed the pink flush in her cheeks as she handed me a large bottle of white paint.

"They won't work for the kids' tables," she said, her voice trembling.

"They're empty? Or dry?" I asked.

"Oh no," she said, shaking her head. "They're brand new." She handed me the bottle.

Bruno, curious, gave it a good sniff. I let him investigate, and after a few moments, he settled by my feet. I made a mental note to ask Logan about that—probably part of Bruno's training, though I had no idea what it meant.

Art, Vendors and Forgery

"They're permanent acrylics," Sophie continued. "I don't think parents will be thrilled if we hand those to their kids."

Sandie and I exchanged a look.

"You're right, Sophie," I said. "Not ideal. Just buy the washable kind, and we'll store them with the rest of our supplies."

"That's the thing," Sophie said. "I tried to return them, but there's no record of purchase or donation. I don't think the city owns them."

"Well, that's strange," I said. "How many bottles are we talking?"

"Two sets of twelve. All liter-sized."

Bert gave a low whistle. "That can't be cheap. Maybe someone from the community center events forgot them?"

That wasn't the problem. The issue wasn't *if* they belonged to the city—it was *where* they were found and *when*. Something about it didn't sit right with me, but I couldn't quite put my finger on it.

"Don't worry, I'll look into it. Just leave them in my office when you head back."

Chapter 21

I parked by the museum's entrance with Sandie, and despite the spring sunshine, a shiver crept down my spine. The last time I'd been here, the museum had turned into a crime scene. I just hoped coming back didn't mean stumbling into another killer—like what happened years ago at the tavern.

"Come on," Sandie said, already halfway out of the car. "I'm the one with the enormous belly and swollen ankles, not you."

I could've argued that she wasn't that big for her ankles to bother her—but there was no point. Instead, I hurried after her.

"Hello," I said to the gentleman at the front desk as we stepped inside. "My name is Margaret Willow, and I was hoping to speak with Director Tristan DeVoir."

Art, Vendors and Forgery

The man barely looked up, peering at me over the rim of his readers. "Is he expecting you?"

"No," I said, and just as he opened his mouth—no doubt to send me away—I added, "But I'm the Director of Parks and Recreation for the town of Apple Creek, and I need to speak with someone here about our... um... latest incident."

That got his attention. He adjusted his glasses, exhaled loudly, and replied with a superior air. "Director DeVoir is too busy for anyone without an appointment. If you would like to make one—"

"Oh sure," I said joyfully. I am happy to come back with Fred Roberts. I'm sure he'll be a delightful addition to this conversation."

That did it. He turned his back on us, but picked up the museum's phone.

"Wait... can you actually bring Council member Roberts here?" Sandie whispered.

I didn't have to answer. The man turned back with a stiffer spine and a far less pleasant expression.

"Mr. DeVoir will see you. Do you know where his office is?"

I smiled and looped my arm through Sandie's. "Of course I do. Thanks."

Only then did he seem to notice Bruno at my side. His eyes widened, and he straightened.

"You can't bring the dog inside the museum," he said. "This is a no-animals facility. No exceptions."

I felt Sandie tense beside me, inhaling deeply, but I gave her a quick look to let her know I had this.

"Is that so?" I asked, smiling brightly. "Because according to city code, all facilities providing public services must allow service and companion animals on the premises."

He opened his mouth, but I kept going.

"This museum, being a nonprofit funded through donations and taxpayer money, qualifies as a public service."

He tried again, and this time I raised my hand, wagging my index finger in the air, just shy of his nose.

"And this dog happens to be a K9 officer. Are you trying to obstruct justice? Because I'd be more than happy to call the police and have *you* arrested."

His mouth fell open, but no words came out. He stepped back as the color drained from his face.

I turned and walked off with Sandie. Bruno trotted beside us, and as we passed the desk, he let out a low, deliberate growl. The man gasped and knocked into his chair with a squeak.

"That was awesome," Sandie whispered as we headed down the hallway lined with framed exhibits and dusty plaques.

"You know what would be awesome?" I said, glancing at her. "If we could actually *find* DeVoir's office."

"Maggie!"

Thankfully, Sandie had been to the museum more often than I had and found the director's office with no problem. I might've been here recently, but I hadn't exactly been paying attention to the building. My nerves had been too busy focusing on the fact that there was a dead body lying somewhere inside.

"Miss Willow," Tristan DeVoir called from his doorway. "I hope you didn't get lost. It's a big house."

"Indeed, it is," I said, stepping into his office. "This is my sister, Sandie Willow—and I'm not sure if you've met Officer Bruno yet."

I gestured to Bruno, partly out of habit, partly because I'd already noticed the director casting disapproving glances at my furry partner.

"A pleasure to meet you," DeVoir said, shaking Sandie's hand a little too quickly. "What can I do for you ladies? As you can imagine, recent events have thrown off my schedule—I don't have the luxury of much time."

I took a seat across from his desk while Bruno began his usual routine of sniffing the room. Oddly, he didn't settle down right away. I wished—not for the first time—that I could read his mind.

"Does he have to walk around like that?" DeVoir asked, frowning. "This is a historical furniture set, and I'd hate for his drool to damage it."

Sandie shifted uncomfortably in her chair—an early warning sign that she was ready to start a debate.

"Mr. DeVoir," she said, "would you interrupt a police officer while he was conducting an investigation?"

"If he didn't have a warrant? Yes, I would," DeVoir said, settling into his chair with a smug smile.

Sandie huffed, but I didn't let it rattle me. After years of navigating passive-aggressive city

Art, Vendors and Forgery

council meetings, I'd picked up a few tricks of my own.

"In that case, you're more than welcome to stop him," I said calmly.

"But... isn't this *your* dog?" he asked, and for a moment, I noticed his strange accent vanish entirely, and I remembered Bert said a guy with a thick accent rang the office on the day of the murder.

. "He could bite me."

I shrugged. "I co-own him, sure. But I'm not his boss. That would be Chief Forest—and he's not here. You can try to stop him if you like, but if he bites you... well, I think that counts as an arrest."

DeVoir blanched, then quickly recovered, the accent sliding back into place like a mask. "Let's get to the point, shall we?" he said, straightening his cuffs. "I believe it's obvious we will *not* be allowing any of our paintings to be part of the carnival. After what happened, the board is panicked, and the insurance agency won't even return our calls."

"Well, that's interesting," Sandie said, matching his tone with one of her own. "Considering the robbery happened on *your* property. The security failure was yours—not the fault of the R-Parks Department or the city."

DeVoir shifted in his seat, his features hardening. "The painting never would've been at risk if the city hadn't insisted on showcasing it. Maintaining these pieces comes at a cost, and when problems like this arise, we *all* lose."

"Wouldn't the publicity bring more curious visitors to the museum?" I asked.

"Perhaps. But the minimal price of a ticket doesn't come close to covering what it takes to maintain this building, the restoration lab, the temperature-controlled rooms... It's more than we could ever make in admissions."

I saw Sandie's eyes widen—she was about to say something that might burn a bridge. So I jumped in without really thinking.

"A Rodriguez is worth hundreds of thousands, right? Wouldn't the insurance payout cover your costs for a while?"

DeVoir sniffed and lifted his chin. "*If* the painting were missing."

The second the words left his mouth, he froze. Sandie's sharp gasp confirmed he'd said more than he meant to.

"You recovered the painting?" she asked.

He stood quickly, stepping away from his desk—but Bruno blocked him. The dog didn't growl, didn't lunge—he just stood there, quiet

Art, Vendors and Forgery

and immovable, like the world's fluffiest bouncer.

DeVoir hesitated, then slowly returned to his seat, placing his hands on the desk. "That is classified information," he said tightly. "I hope you understand that I can't disclose anything further."

He looked trapped. Desperate. And, thankfully, not armed. I leaned in.

"I'm sure Maple Hollow will be thrilled to hear they'll get the Rodriguez after all."

"Maple Hollow?" DeVoir chuckled with that condescending tilt of his head. "If you believe that woman's story, you're more naïve than I thought. Why would I send our most valuable painting to another city? I didn't want to lend it *down the street*, let alone *miles away*."

He stood again, signaling the conversation was over.

"I really must get back to work. But don't worry, Miss Willow. I'm sure you'll enjoy the museum's annual donation to the carnival. Someone already dropped it off at your... gathering spot."

I stood too, watching as he shook Sandie's hand. Confused, I asked, "Annual donation?"

"Of course," he said, turning to offer his hand to me. "You're new to town—you'll catch on. As long as those kids enjoy the paintings," —he smiled—"that's all that matters."

As he spoke, a bright blue stain on his palm caught my attention. He noticed my gaze and quickly added, "It's all dry. I was working on a painting this morning. You know—artist's life."

The second I closed the car door, Sandie spun in her seat, eyes wide and eyebrows practically touching her hairline.

"He was talking about the paint bottles your people were discussing in the park, right?" she whispered, as if anyone could hear us inside my locked car.

I nodded, clicking my seatbelt into place. "That's what he said. But you heard Sophie—there's no record of anything being donated."

"Well, probably because it's such a lame donation," Sandie said, slipping back into her regular voice. "I mean, who makes a big deal over a few bottles of acrylics? Not exactly priceless, and totally useless for the festival. And by the way," she added, frowning and air-quoting, "'*a carnival*'? He said that on purpose. Just to make you mad."

"I don't think he likes being questioned..." I murmured. "What do you think about the painting?"

"He's totally lying," she replied without missing a beat, buckling her seatbelt. "I think he *was* planning to send the painting to Maple Hollow, and Mrs. Roberts figured it out. She probably tried to use the art festival as a way to keep the painting in town."

From the backseat, Bruno sat up straight, eyes locked on the museum building. If I had to guess, I'd say DeVoir was watching us from his office window. The thought sent a cold shiver down my spine.

"I don't know," I said to Sandie as I slowly backed out of the parking spot, trying not to look too paranoid. "He clearly didn't want us to know they recovered the painting. And he didn't seem happy to have it back. Do you think the museum's finances are that bad?"

Sandie scoffed. "I doubt it. Paul's company was here last fall and remodeled their greenhouse and patio. I figured they'd use it for events, like the country club, but nope! Lucy wanted it for her wedding, and they said it's just for *'private art gatherings'*. Whatever that means."

"A big remodel?"

"Oh, yeah. Water mirrors and everything. It must be glorious. But it's private."

As we drove back to the park, I started putting the pieces together—and I realized what I needed to do next. I just really didn't want to do it. And I definitely needed Sandie's skills for this one.

"Sandie, I need to talk to Dana," I mumbled.

Her head whipped toward me. "*Dana?* Well, *that* is something I need to see."

"That won't happen," I warned.

Sandie threw her arms up. "Why not? I could be helpful, you know. I can stop you from killing her."

"You can help me *find* her," I offered instead, knowing it wouldn't go over well.

Her face soured. "Just ask the traitor—sorry, *Forest*. I'm sure he knows."

When I didn't jump to defend Logan, or even respond, she turned more fully toward me, her voice softening.

"You don't want him to know?"

I let out a long sigh and nodded.

"Margaret Willow!" she scolded. "What are

Art, Vendors and Forgery

you going to ask? Remember, you don't go digging for answers you don't want to hear. They may have been married, but they're not anymore. That's what matters."

"What?" I frowned. "I'm not asking about their marriage, Sandie. I need to know about the painting and the museum. Logan won't let me ask what I really need to—he's always defending her. I need to talk to Dana alone. Without him knowing."

She turned back in her seat and crossed her arms. "And how exactly can I help you with that?"

I tried my best Darcy impression—the wide eyes, the desperate little smile. "Can you find out where she is? I know she's under house arrest, but I don't know where she's living now... *please*?"

"And how am I supposed to get her address?"

I parked next to her car and turned to her with a big grin. "You've got your ways. Like Mom."

Sandie narrowed her eyes, clearly unimpressed, and climbed out of the car. "Fine. But it won't be easy, Maggie."

"Thanks, beautiful sister!"

She waved off the compliment and asked, "Aren't you coming?"

"I have to stop by the tavern and pick up someone's lunch. I need to prove a point."

Sandie chuckled and shut the door. I rolled the window down and called out, "I'll bring you a slice of cheesecake later!"

She gave me a thumbs-up with an extra-bright smile and headed toward the park.

I looked back at Bruno. "All right, partner. Let's go get Linda some food."

Chapter 22

Cyder's Pub during the day wasn't the same loud chaos the night crowd brought. It was quieter, more relaxed —but the delicious smell of food lingered, warm and comforting. My stomach rumbled in protest, reminding me I hadn't eaten since breakfast. At this point, I wasn't sure if I was grabbing lunch or an early dinner.

"Afternoon," a guy behind the bar greeted as I stepped inside. "What can I get for you?"

"Could I take a look at the menu, please?"

He smiled and handed me the familiar, slightly sticky laminated list. I could've ordered from memory, but since I was picking something up for Linda, I figured it was best to browse.

"I thought I recognized that voice," Mr.

Elliot called out as he came from the kitchen, wiping his hands on a dish towel. "How are you doing, Maggie?"

It was always a comfort to see Mr. Elliot. No matter how long or bad the day was, he had a way of making things feel lighter.

Bruno clearly felt the same—he sprang up, landing his front paws squarely on Mr. Elliot's chest and nearly knocking the poor man back a step.

"I missed you too, pal!" he laughed.

"Bruno! Down!" I scolded, though he ignored me, as usual. Mr. Elliot was the one who gently nudged him back down.

"My fault," he said, giving Bruno a final scratch behind the ears. "I should've greeted him first."

Then his face turned serious. "Any news on Ben or Dana?"

I shook my head. "Nothing solid. Just that Mrs. Roberts and Dana are under house arrest... and Ben's still at the station."

Mr. Elliot sighed. "Man, I hope they don't send him to county jail. He put away a lot of bad folks in there."

"My mom's worried about that too," I admitted.

"She must be a wreck. I'm sending her some soup—it might help, you never know."

I smiled as he disappeared back into the kitchen. The bartender came over to take my order, and I sat down to wait, my mind still spinning from our visit to the museum.

DeVoir was hiding something. Or at the very least, he was playing with the truth. What bothered me was how he mentioned the museum's financial struggles now, but when he and Mrs. Roberts spoke to the Mayor, he never brought that up. Even if ticket sales weren't bringing in much, attracting visitors was how you secured donors. That's just how it worked.

"You didn't like him much, huh, Bruno?" I said.

He looked up, ears perking—but I could tell his attention was fixed on the treat Mr. Elliot had sent out for him. Figures.

Those supposed donated paints crept back into my thoughts. Why mention that silly donation? Was he mocking the festival? Or was there more to it?

"Here you go," Mr. Elliot said, returning with a paper bag. "Your mom's soup is at the bottom. I added a treat for you, too."

"Oooh, now I'm intrigued. Thank you!"

"Absolutely. Hope you're back soon with

that little cutie. I've got cookie samples that need testing."

"Cookie samples?" I raised a brow. "I volunteer as tribute."

He chuckled, turning back toward the kitchen—then paused, reaching into his pocket.

"Here," he said, handing me a worn leather wallet. "Found this under a table this morning. I should take it to the station, but... well, Ben won't be able to pick it up himself. And I figured your mom might be the first person he wants to see when he gets out."

I held the wallet for a second, the gesture unexpectedly warming my chest. "I'll give it to her."

I was halfway to the door when a thought stopped me cold. I turned back. "When was Ben here?"

Mr. Elliot looked up, his mouth tilting thoughtfully. "Three... maybe four days ago. He had dinner. Dana was with him. Then a guy in a fancy suit came and sat down with them."

My eyes narrowed. "A guy in a fancy suit?"

He nodded. "Yeah. Looked out of place in here, you know? I didn't think much of it at the time..." He trailed off with a shrug. "I just

Art, Vendors and Forgery

hope this mess clears up," Mr. Elliot added. "Good people, both of them. They don't belong in the middle of something like this."

I gave him a grateful smile and slipped out the door, my thoughts racing faster than my feet. Now I had a pretty good idea of how Ben lost my mom's photo. And I had an even better reason to talk to Dana.

After dropping off Linda's late lunch—and enjoying her surprise to see me back—I pushed through some paperwork at the office. Or at least, I tried. My thoughts kept looping around the case: Ben, the museum, the lost wallet, and that man in the fancy suit. I couldn't concentrate on what I was signing, and that's never a good thing when you're the director of a city department, so I left early.

It was still early evening when I opened the front door and paused in the entryway. My mom stood beside a whiteboard, and my sweet five-year-old was happily scribbling on it—lines, arrows, and something that might've been a smiley face... or a suspect.

"Are you teaching Darcy how to build a

crime board, Mom?" I asked, half amused, half curious.

My mom jumped a little, then chuckled. "Mainly teaching her how to spell names, Maggie. Just getting her ready for kindergarten."

Darcy turned and bolted into my arms. "You're home! I missed you!"

I wrapped her in a tight hug, pressing a kiss to her forehead. "I missed you too, sunflower."

Then Bruno joined in, leaping into the mix like he'd been waiting his turn. Suddenly I was on the floor—forgotten in the middle of a giggling, tail-wagging whirlwind.

My mom offered me a hand and helped me up.

"I guess she has a new favorite," I said, brushing fur and crumbs off my clothes.

"Well," she smirked, "now you know how *I* felt when you left me for that silly fish of yours."

I snorted. "Hardly the same. The fish didn't leap on me every time I checked their filter."

Instead of bantering further, I gave her a more serious look. "How are you holding up?"

She sighed and sank onto the couch, giving the board a tired glance. "Good, I suppose. I keep telling myself Ben's been gone for years

Art, Vendors and Forgery

and this shouldn't feel like my responsibility anymore, but..." She pointed to the chaotic web of names and arrows. "Apparently, my brain disagrees."

I sat beside her and reached into my bag. "Mr. Elliot asked me to give this to you," I said, handing her Ben's wallet. "I guess you're not the only one who thinks the past still matters."

Her hands closed around the wallet like it was made of glass. "I wish he'd told me he was coming back to town," she said quietly. "Then at least I wouldn't have to add that to my suspicions."

I looked at the whiteboard. It was... a lot. Names stretched from the Mayor to Chief Anderson's wife, and even one arrow that might've looped toward the PTA.

"Mom," I said slowly, "I'm surprised my name's not on there. Do you really think the Mayor worked with the Chief's wife to get Deputy Warren to frame himself for murder... just to pin it on Ben?"

She gave a short laugh and pushed a stray hair behind her ear. "I don't know what to think anymore. Just be grateful I didn't put the president on there. It *did* cross my mind."

I laughed, the tension breaking just a little.

"You're not alone in overthinking things," I said, standing.

"Where are you going?"

"To my car—I forgot your soup."

I didn't want to go over my day. I didn't want to hear how many times she and my sister had called me that morning. It wasn't necessary. I already felt like my brain was a shaken snow globe, with too many pieces swirling around and none of them settling into place.

"Miss Willow," a male voice said behind my car, making me jump and bump my head on the car door.

"Ow—" I clutched my head, biting back a few choice words.

"I'm so sorry," the voice said quickly. "I didn't mean to scare you... again."

As I rubbed the sore spot and turned around, I found Deputy Warren standing a few steps back, notebook and pen in hand. He looked serious, all business as usual, but there was something softer about his expression tonight. His shoulders sagged a little, like the

Art, Vendors and Forgery

weight of the day—or maybe the week—was finally catching up to him.

"Deputy Warren. How can I help you?"

He cleared his throat. "I stopped by your office, but you were gone. Mrs. Oak mentioned your phone wasn't working properly today, so I took the liberty of interrupting your evening."

I knew what Logan had said about Warren. I'd heard him loud and clear. But it was hard to connect those warnings with the polite, quietly intense man standing in front of me.

"Please, don't worry. I probably *should* still be working," I said, gesturing for him to walk with me back toward the house. "Would you like some tea?"

As I opened the front door, Bruno charged down the hallway like he was greeting a long-lost friend. He launched himself at Deputy Warren, tail wagging in delight.

The deputy crouched down, laughing softly as he scratched behind Bruno's ears. "Hey, buddy. Miss me already?"

My mom, on the other hand, stood up from the couch and crossed her arms with a glare sharp enough to slice through caution tape.

"Did you come to arrest my daughter now?"

"Mom!" I hissed.

Deputy Warren looked between the two of us, not missing a beat. "Absolutely not, Mrs. Willow. I'm here because I need your daughter's expertise and knowledge."

Then his gaze drifted to the whiteboard behind her. My face flushed. Oh no. If anything was clear from that mess of arrows and names, it was that my mom had made him her prime suspect.

"That's an interesting theory," he said lightly.

My mom turned to look at the board, then back at him. "We were just... working on spelling with my granddaughter."

I rolled my eyes. "With a marker and a crime web?"

Warren chuckled beside me. "Next time I visit my nephews, I might try this board idea. Could help with homework."

Then he straightened and flipped open his notebook. "Miss Willow, I noticed the department budget on your desk earlier today. I know you're new, but I wanted to ask a few questions."

I crossed my arms, suddenly feeling like a teenager being called out in class. "To be honest, the budget hasn't exactly had my full attention this week."

He gave a slight smile and nodded. "Understandable. It's been a strange week for all of us."

Only then did I realize just how strange his week must have been. His boss disappeared, leaving him temporarily in charge of the department. Then he landed in the middle of a robbery-homicide investigation that seemed to involve a different former boss. And now the mayor had skipped over him entirely to name a new police chief. Not to mention whatever past involvement Warren might have in this tangled web.

I nodded slowly. "Fair point."

"I wanted to ask about the Recreation and Parks Department's relationship with the museum," he said. "Are there any financial ties?"

I took a deep breath as my mom silently slipped out of the room. "Not that I'm aware of. The only connection I know of is related to the festival and the painting. Maybe there was something in the past. I can check with Mrs. Oak and the City Manager in the morning."

He shook his head. "That won't be necessary. I'll talk to Mr. Norton tomorrow." He scribbled a note, then looked up again. "What about donations for the festival? Do you have any records on those?"

"Actually, yes." I studied him for a moment, catching the rhythm of his questions. "Do you remember the vandalism at the community center?"

He nodded.

"Well, during the cleanup, we found two sets of paint bottles in storage. No one seemed to know where they came from, but this afternoon, when I spoke with Mr. DeVoir, he claimed they were the museum's annual donation."

"And there's no such donation?"

"Not that I've ever seen in our records," I said honestly. "When I asked Mrs. Oak, she wasn't sure about them."

Warren jotted that down, then turned toward the door. "Thank you, Miss Willow."

But he paused just before stepping outside. His hand rested on the doorknob, and I could see the hesitation in his posture. Whatever he was about to say, it felt personal.

I waited.

"Mr. DeVoir mentioned financial trouble at the museum," he said finally. "Had you heard anything about that? Maybe in a city meeting or through... unofficial channels?"

Art, Vendors and Forgery

I leaned on the doorframe, weighing my words. "He mentioned it to me today, but it felt off. The day Mrs. Roberts introduced him to the mayor, he didn't mention a single concern. He was cheerful. Excited to have a professional examine the painting for safety. That doesn't sound like someone budgeting for cutbacks."

Warren nodded slowly, frowning at his notes. "You're right to question him. Unlike with you, I'm not looking forward to our next conversation—but it's on my list. Thanks again for talking to me."

I watched him walk down the driveway, his posture heavy under the streetlight's glow. Bruno sat beside me, his head resting against my leg.

I scratched behind his ears. "So... you like him? Yeah, I think I do too. But let's keep that between us."

Chapter 23

I *knew* something was off the moment Sandie told me over the phone not to overreact. Still, as I parked outside Logan's apartment, I couldn't believe I was actually doing this. Even if it was the perfect chance to talk to Dana, it felt reckless.

According to Sandie, Dana had been staying with Logan ever since she was placed under house arrest. A peculiar arrangement, considering she was a criminal and he was a detective. Luckily, he'd never been the ambitious type—otherwise this would've been a full-blown scandal.

I expected a long conversation with Dana through the intercom. Paul had told Sandie he saw Logan walking with the Mayor after dropping off some supplies at the community center. He overheard the Mayor mentioning last-minute reports, which made me think Logan would be out for a while. Still, when the door buzzed open with no questions asked, my anxiety spiked.

The last time I'd been here was just a week ago—Logan had asked me to drop off Bruno overnight since he had an early case and didn't want to bother my mom or Darcy. That time, climbing the steps had felt natural. This time, Bruno tugged on the leash like he was eager to get inside while my stomach twisted into knots. I didn't want to see Logan. And I *really* didn't want to see Dana. But I had no choice.

"I told you to grab your keys," Dana muttered as she opened the door. "I guess some things never—"

She stopped cold when she saw me. "—never change?" I finished for her.

She leaned against the doorframe, her tone immediately deflated. "I have nothing to say to you."

Bruno didn't care. He jumped up on the door, forcing her to step back, then trotted inside like he owned the place. He hopped onto the couch and curled up like it was still his home.

Dana groaned and walked into the living

room. "Logan's not here. If you're dropping off Bruno, fine—but *you* better walk him before you leave. I'm not doing it."

Bruno whined softly, his ears drooping. My dislike for Dana only deepened.

"I bet you different," I said, stepping inside before she could slam the door in my face. "Why did the Rodriguez end up in your office?"

Her face drained of color, and the smugness slipped away. All that was left was fear.

"No," she whispered, backing up to lean against the couch. "The painting was stolen. It got stolen. Why would it be in my—oh no. This is bad. Really bad."

If she was faking, she deserved an award—but I doubted she had the talent. "It *is* bad, Dana. But you know more than you're saying. I need the whole story. All of it."

She closed her eyes and covered her face. Her breathing grew ragged, and for a second, I almost felt bad for her. *Almost.* Then she opened her mouth.

"That Mrs. Roberts is plotting against me. She did it, but since she's your buddy, you won't see it."

I rolled my eyes. "Let's say Mrs. Roberts *did* do it. What proof do you have?"

Art, Vendors and Forgery

"Isn't it obvious? Her obsession with that painting? How she kept pushing Tristan to put it in the middle of the park? That woman was going to steal it the moment we moved it from the museum."

"So when DeVoir decided to send it to Maple Hollow, she hatched a plan to use the entire art festival as a cover—and killed the one man who could approve her request?"

"There you go," she said, as if she'd solved it.

I smiled thinly and sat down at the table. "The only problem is that *none* of that lines up with the facts, Dana. For example, your *lover* was the curator of the painting, and he happened to have a rare condition that made him vulnerable to ingesting poison. And you contacted Ben—not just on the day of the murder, but the night before, at Cyder's Pub—with another man. Someone well-dressed. Maybe Scott?"

Her hands trembled. "That has nothing to do with this. I can't—Logan will fix it. Ben will walk free and—"

"And Mrs. Roberts takes the blame? Dana! What's going on? Who are you afraid of?"

She clamped her mouth shut and crossed her arms.

"Did Logan tell you about Warren finding a photo of my mom dedicated to Ben at the crime scene?"

Tears welled up in her eyes and she bit her lip. "So you're okay with Ben rotting in prison? I'm sure the guys he put behind bars will welcome him with open arms."

A soft cry escaped her lips, which she quickly covered.

"And what about Scott? Don't you want to know who *really* killed him—or do you already know?"

She burst into tears. Between sobs, she corrected me.

"It wasn't Scott with us in the tavern. It was Tristan."

I didn't have time to process that before she continued.

"You're right, Scott was involved—but not the way you think. That painting required some retouching a few years ago, a job handled by Scott. After that job, Scott became our curator. After Rodriguez died, his art became more valuable. When I told Scott about Mrs. Roberts' plan, he freaked out. Said he'd go to jail and when he explained everything to me... well, I panicked."

She sat down on the couch beside Bruno.

Art, Vendors and Forgery

"I called Ben because... well, Logan and I weren't on good terms. Ben was the only cop I trusted. He asked to meet at the tavern, but we didn't talk much—Tristan was there, and I didn't want my boss finding out."

I leaned forward. "What did Scott confess?"

"The painting was a *fake*," Dana whispered, resting her head against the couch. "It's a big crime. And he knew it when he worked on it. Said he needed the money. But now Rodriguez is more famous, and a fake painting means a scandal. It put Scott in a bigger trouble."

She stared into the distance. "I just wanted to understand what Scott was facing. I needed to find out what would happen if he came clean. I felt like an accomplice... just a poorer one."

Part of me got it—but it wasn't fair for Ben or Mrs. Roberts to take the fall.

"Ben told you to go to the police," I said, and she nodded.

"What else did he say?"

"Not much. Tristan showed up. But Ben said Scott could make a deal if he named the person who paid him off. Later that night, Scott got furious when I told him I talked to

Ben. He said I'd put my life in danger. Wouldn't say who paid him—just that they were powerful. I've never seen him like that." She swallowed hard. "And now he's dead."

Bruno rested his head on her lap, comforting her in a way I couldn't. I still had questions. Ben's freedom mattered more than her tears.

"That's why you think Mrs. Roberts did it?"

Dana looked up, eyes sharp. "She's your friend, but she's evil. Why else demand that painting after Rodriguez died?"

"Maybe she just wanted to honor the artist," I countered.

Dana scoffed.

"How did the painting end up in your office?" I asked.

"I don't know. But it doesn't matter now."

"I'm sure a *fake* doesn't have value but—"

"It's not just that." She stood up, stormed into another room, and I heard her rummaging through boxes. A few minutes later, she returned, arms full. Bruno sprang off the couch to investigate.

"Out of the way!" she yelled, trying to get past him.

Art, Vendors and Forgery

"What's in the box?" I asked, holding Bruno back by his collar.

"My art supplies—and this." She pulled out a bottle of acrylic paint. It looked just like the ones we found at the community center. Bruno sniffed it eagerly.

Dana ignored him. "Scott came that day into my office. We tried calling your department, but it was no use. No one knew anything there. He got all flustered and said he'd *fixed* it. He used that paint—he covered the sky."

"He painted over the *Rodriguez*?"

"Stress made his condition worse. I ran to the exhibit and saw what he did. I called Ben. Then I went looking for Scott and... found him on the ground. I didn't even notice the painting was gone until you and Mrs. Roberts showed up." Her voice dropped to a whisper. "I have no idea how it ended up in my office."

I left Logan's apartment more concerned than when I entered, but almost certain that Dana was innocent. I had never doubted Ben, and now I knew why he'd come back—and how his wallet had gone missing. If Scott's accomplice had followed Dana, they could have easily taken my mom's photo and planted it at the scene.

Mrs. Roberts just didn't add up. Sure, she had a magnificent private art collection, but she could have bought the painting from the museum—especially if the finances were in bad shape. I mentally cursed myself for not asking Dana about that. She must be aware of any financial issues, if there were any.

Deputy Warren's name popped up on my dashboard screen, which was both alarming and unusual. It was late now, and if he had been apologetic before, this had to be an emergency.

"Hello?" I answered, but all I heard was white noise. "Hello? Deputy Warren?"

I figured he had just bumped his phone or pocket-dialed me and was about to hang up when I heard a distorted voice through the static.

"Big mistake—alone—bad choice—"

The white noise swallowed the rest. I couldn't make out the words. A scream of pain followed by a loud crash ended the call.

"Hello!" I shouted at my car, immediately feeling foolish. "As if the criminal was going to pick up my call now."

Art, Vendors and Forgery

I hung up and turned my car around. I remembered our previous conversation, which told me exactly where he was... or so I hope.

The museum was less than five minutes away. The police station was at least fifteen, and I had no idea if there were any patrols closer. While I drove, I called Logan, but when he didn't answer after the second ring, I hung up and called 911.

"What's your emergency?" a very calm voice asked.

"Deputy Warren is in danger!" I shouted, ignoring whatever else she tried to say. "He's at the History Museum—someone may be killing him! You need to send the police there. Now!"

"Miss, could you please give me your name and let me know how you know—"

I ran a red light and turned onto the museum's street. "My name is Margaret Willow. I'm the director of R-Parks. He called me—well, misdialed. I heard someone threatening him and then a loud crash."

As I pulled into the parking lot, I turned on my high beams and honked repeatedly. Maybe someone nearby would call 911 too. Although that was wishful thinking—the museum sat at the end of the street, surrounded mostly by parks.

I definitely wasn't expecting Bruno to leap out the window and sprint into the museum.

"Bruno!" I yelled, but it was too late. I knew I should've stayed by my car, but that was my dog—and I wasn't going to leave him alone with a murderer.

I locked my car, set off the alarm to keep the noise going, and ran toward the entrance. Everything was pitch black. I turned on my phone's flashlight as a shiver ran down my spine, stirring memories of the ice arena from a few weeks ago.

Inside, I slowed my steps, trying to control my heartbeat and my spiraling thoughts.

Warren must have been close to the truth. Otherwise, why would he be in danger? He hadn't seemed happy about dealing with De-Voir again. For a moment, I hesitated. Maybe Warren wasn't even in the museum and I'd made a huge mistake. But then—why had Bruno run in here like that?

The answer hit me like a flash.

Bruno had been trying to tell me something all along. He was drawn to the paint bottles in the park—probably because he remembered the scent from Dana's art set. As much as it pained me to think about, Bruno

Art, Vendors and Forgery

must've lived with Logan when he was married to Dana.

I shook my head and focused. Bruno had been sniffing around DeVoir earlier, and his hand had a blue stain—just like the sky in the Rodriguez painting. He must have tried to paint over whatever Scott did. DeVoir had the connections and the resources—and he ran the museum. He had to know the painting was fake. That's why he wasn't pleased when the police recovered it.

My phone rang, startling me so much I nearly dropped it. Seeing Logan's name made me breathe a little easier.

"DeVoir is behind it," I whispered as I answered, nearly blinding myself with my flashlight.

"Maggie!" he shouted. From the noise in the background, I guessed he was close to the museum. "Where are you?"

I covered my phone and leaned in closer. "Bruno ran inside. I couldn't leave him alone."

He groaned and said something that wasn't directed at me. "Listen to me," he said so loudly I worried someone inside the museum might hear. "Bruno will be fine. This is his job. You need to get out of there. Now."

My face flushed. Of course it was ridiculous

221

to think I needed to save Bruno—he was a trained police dog. But I didn't have time to feel embarrassed.

"You'd better put that down," a voice said behind me, followed by something sharp pressing into my back. "Drop it."

A heavy boot crushed my phone. I was spun around roughly by the shoulders.

"Miss Willow," DeVoir sneered, "you should have been grateful for my donation and left the matter alone."

His expression wasn't triumphant—it was panicked. The gun in his hand glinted as he gestured for me to move ahead of him.

Chapter 24

The second DeVoir opened the door, the strong smell of paint and solvents hit me. Somehow, it reminded me of Sandie's room, and I wondered how something so comforting could mix so horribly with fear.

I looked around—no sign of Bruno. Oddly enough, I felt relieved. In my mind, he was still my dog, not an officer. Then I saw the body of who I guessed was Deputy Warren on the ground and tried to step toward it, but DeVoir shoved the gun harder into my back.

"I wouldn't move if I were you," he said, just as I heard bottles clinking and papers rustling behind me. "I was expecting him. Not you. Now I have to improvise."

"The police are surrounding the building. You have no escape."

He laughed, and I turned to look at him. Only then did I notice the latex glove on the hand holding the gun and a glass bottle in the other.

"I'm glad they're here," he said, smiling. "Now I don't even have to figure out how to call for help."

I frowned, and he smirked. "Not so quick, are you? I'm not shocked. Having a high IQ is a curse, Miss Willow. You see all the mistakes everyone makes—and how easily they could've been avoided. Just like chess."

I needed to buy time—and make noise.

"Like chess," I echoed, finally seeing the full picture. "You knew the painting was a fake. You paid Scott years ago. It worked—this museum gained prestige, and you became its director. But then Sebastian died, and his work started to be remembered. Revalued."

He smashed the bottle against the drawing desk, making me jump back with a gasp.

"Almost right," he said, grinning. "Miss Willow, you could've been smarter. But you're too curious. Big mistake."

"The painting was supposed to disappear on its way to Maple Hollow," I pressed. "But Mrs. Roberts interrupted your plan. You had to improvise."

Art, Vendors and Forgery

He pointed the jagged bottle at me and gave it a lazy shake. "Catherine and her nosy little habits. She's the one who forced this. That's why she'll take the fall—along with my useless assistant and that broken cop."

He dragged the broken edge across his arm, and I flinched, looking away. That's when I noticed Deputy Warren's chest rise—faint, but there. A soft groan escaped his lips. He was still alive.

"You killed Scott for not sticking to the lie and ruining the painting," I said, keeping my voice steady. "He had no idea he was drinking poison."

DeVoir chuckled, pleased with himself. "And that drink stank to high heaven, but he deserved it. Falling for that damaged woman, then trying to sabotage me? Not smart."

A shadow moved behind him, but I didn't react. If that was Bruno, I didn't want him leaping while DeVoir still had a gun pointed at me and a broken bottle in his other hand.

"The best part," DeVoir said, "was watching Dana's eyes nearly pop out when she saw me at the tavern. I'll say this—your mother's a very good-looking woman. I might pay her a visit. Offer my condolences for your loss."

"You stole Ben's wallet!" I snapped. "He didn't do anything to you. Why—?"

"Dana called him," DeVoir shrugged. "She got him involved. It worked. It distracted the sleepy officer behind you. But hey... collateral damage. Just like you."

I heard footsteps approaching, and DeVoir stepped closer.

"I'll fill you in—since you won't be alive to see it. Warren trapped me and dragged me here, trying to frame me for his earlier crime. You walked in, playing amateur detective—very irresponsible, by the way—and he shot you. While you were down, we fought. I killed him. Self-defense." He smacked his lips. "Hey, at least you'll die knowing your cop friend walks free."

I didn't have time to argue or process whether that ridiculous plan could even work.

Something crashed near the door. DeVoir spun around, aiming his gun. A shadow leapt from behind, tackling him to the ground. A shot rang out, followed by a loud growl and a clatter of bodies hitting the floor.

I jumped up, grabbed the first thing I could —an unopened bottle of solvent—and rushed toward the commotion. Bruno stood on one side, growling low and steady, his fur bristling

Art, Vendors and Forgery

as he blocked DeVoir's path. On the other side, Logan was pale, one hand clutched tightly over his shoulder.

"Get back!" Logan yelled as he kicked DeVoir, making him drop the broken bottle. But I saw the gun lifting.

Without thinking, I smashed the bottle against DeVoir's head. His face hit the floor with a thud, and the gun slipped from his grasp. Bruno lunged, pinning him down with a fierce growl.

"Are you okay?" Logan asked from the floor. My stomach dropped as I saw the blood covering his hand.

"You got shot!" I shouted, jumping up and running out of the workshop. "We need help!" I yelled toward the other officers already rushing in.

Back inside, I turned on the lights and knelt beside Logan, but he wouldn't let me near his shoulder.

"Is he okay?" he asked.

I realizing I'd forgotten about Warren. I rushed to him and exhaled with relief when I saw he was still breathing. I grabbed a clean cloth from a nearby table and placed it under his neck.

Moments later, the paramedics came

227

storming in, and I backed away, feeling equal parts useless and overwhelmingly grateful.

I kept petting Bruno while I sat in the hospital's waiting room. His head rested on my knee, warm and steady, and I was beyond grateful he was allowed to stay with me—as a K9 officer, he had special privileges. Without him, the silence and the sterile air would've been too much.

It felt silly, sitting there when I didn't even know if Logan would be discharged or kept overnight. His family was in Florida, his ex-wife was still under house arrest, and the closest thing he had to a relative was the dog curled up at my feet.

My mom had offered to come, but I convinced her I was fine and asked her to stay with Darcy. It was the middle of the night. There was no reason to wake up the whole family. Besides, once the dust settled, everyone would know the truth.

Across from me sat Deputy Warren's daughter and her husband. She looked to be around my age, and from the red rims of her

Art, Vendors and Forgery

eyes and the crumpled tissue in her hands, she'd been crying since she got there.

A few hours earlier—when time still felt like something I could track—she struck up a quiet conversation with me. Maybe she needed the distraction, or maybe she saw something in me that made her trust me.

"He wasn't always like this," she'd whispered. "So... by-the-book and aggressive. When my mom got sick, something changed. He was forced to slow down. To take care of her. And somehow that changed how he saw people too."

I'd listened, not expecting the ache that bloomed in my chest.

"She told him once that all his rigid rules didn't make life easier. Just lonelier. Before she passed... he promised her he'd try to be better. Kinder. Chief Anderson met him at a family support group and gave him another chance."

I understood why people hesitated around him, but I didn't see it myself because I met him afterward. I noticed the layers. The grief. The growth. The weight he carried. Bruno of course knew, though.

When the doctor finally told her he was stable and would recover, I felt a rush of relief —not just for her, but for the part of me that believed people could change. That second chances weren't just stories.

"*Maggie.*"

Logan's voice pulled me back to the present like a switch flipping inside my chest. I jumped.

Bruno did too, only with joy—his tail wagging wildly as he sprang up and planted his front paws gently on Logan's leg. A nurse pushed him in a wheelchair, his left arm wrapped and resting in a sling.

"What are you doing here?" Logan asked, his tone caught somewhere between confusion and annoyance.

I won't lie—it stung. Something small inside me clenched. But I forced a smile and offered the only answer that didn't feel too vulnerable.

"Well... I didn't know who was going to take you home."

He chuckled softly and scratched Bruno behind the ears. "I think Tricia's waiting outside. The station sent a patrol."

I hadn't even considered that. Of course they would. And before I said something I'd regret, I turned back to Warren's daughter.

"I hope your dad gets better soon."

Art, Vendors and Forgery

She surprised me by standing and hugging me. "Thanks."

No further words. Just that. Then she returned to her seat.

When I turned back, the nurse and Logan were already gone. A knot tightened in my throat before I could stop it. I reached down and buried my fingers in Bruno's fur, using his soft coat as an excuse to steady myself. Just a moment. Just to breathe. I was an adult. I should've known better than to let it get to me—but it did.

The night air outside felt like a blessing—cool and grounding after the too-bright, too-quiet hospital corridors.

I'd just settled Bruno into the passenger seat when a police car pulled up. I waved at Tricia and watched Logan slowly ease out of the front passenger seat.

"I didn't mean to sound..." he started, his voice low. "Well, I'm sorry. I just wasn't expecting to see you there."

There it was again—that small jab. That push that said *we're not really close, are we?*

I looked away. It was easier than admitting how much it hurt.

"Or maybe," he added, "you just felt guilty about what happened?"

"Excuse me?"

"This may be the medicine talking, but didn't you go behind my back? Talk to Dana after I asked you not to? Then, of course, you went and got yourself tangled in something dangerous *again*."

I looked at his arm, guilt threading its way through my chest. But what was I supposed to do—sit back and knit until he was ready to listen?

"You know DeVoir isn't talking," he said. "We still don't know the full story with that painting. The break-ins. The murder."

He opened his mouth, but I beat him to it, voice sharper now.

"I'm sorry you got shot, Logan. I really am. But maybe *you* should remember how many times I tried to get you to take the vandalism at the community center seriously." I said as I walked over to the driver's side and opened the door. "It was all connected—to Durst, to the Rodriguez. But you brushed it off."

He opened his mouth, but Tricia's giggled interrupted him.

"Whose side are you on?" he asked in a nicer tone.

Tricia pretended to seal her lips with his finger.

Art, Vendors and Forgery

"You also asked for my help, Forest," he shook his head. "You did. Against my mom's wishes. Now who is in trouble?"

I didn't wait for him to answer. I was done arguing, done being the one left hanging. This time, I was taking the last word—whether he liked it or not. I yanked the car door open, climbed in, and slammed it shut harder than I meant to.

Chapter 25

The reason I was standing at Catherine Roberts' door was to satisfy my curiosity—and to prove the theory that had kept me awake for the last few nights.

"Maggie!" Catherine opened the door with a warm smile and wrapped her arms around me. "I'm so glad to see you." She pulled back, her voice catching. "I owe you my freedom... everything."

Mrs. Roberts welcomed me in, and I didn't take it lightly. I only hoped that by the end of this visit, I'd still be welcome here.

"I need to ask you a favor," I said, stopping her in her tracks.

"Absolutely, honey. What can I do for you?"

I tried to remain calm, but the mix of

Art, Vendors and Forgery

nerves and excitement was bubbling just beneath the surface. Once Warren was strong enough to identify DeVoir as his attacker, the case was closed. DeVoir confessed to the murder of Scott Durst and how he planted the tampered painting in Dana's office. He apparently left Durst there to die, grabbed the painting, and then snuck in Dana's office after she walked to the gallery. However, he insisted he had no idea how the forged Rodriguez painting got to the museum.

People often said I had a knack for clues, but this was the first time I was chasing one completely on my own. It felt personal—and terrifying.

"Well," I said. "I'm a little worried about the candlelight dinner. Everyone's convinced it's going to rain, and we don't have a backup plan."

Catherine narrowed her eyes. "And let me guess—you have a solution in mind?"

I couldn't help the smile that slipped out. "I think so. The museum renovation. My brother-in-law did the work, and I've heard only amazing things. I know it's reserved for art events, but I was wondering if you could talk to the board. Maybe we could use the space?"

She threw her hands up, eyes shining. "Absolutely! What a marvelous idea! In fact, why not move the entire dinner to the museum's patio? If it rains, they can move everything inside. If it doesn't, well, those guests are in for a treat."

Then her expression shifted, her voice darkening. "DeVoir insisted on making the space exclusive. But now that the truth is out—and with the board knowing what their dear director tried to do to me—they won't be able to say no."

She smiled again and motioned toward the kitchen. "Wonderful thinking, Maggie. This festival is going to be unforgettable. Come, let's have some tea."

"Thank you, Catherine. Actually..." I hesitated, "I was also hoping we could include some fine art in the festival. I loved your idea of featuring local artists—especially Sebastian Rodriguez."

Just as I expected, she froze. When she turned to face me, all the color had drained from her cheeks.

"But the painting was a fake," she whispered. "Who knows what that monster did to the real one."

I took a few steps back until I stood near the door of that dark room in her house. "Yes,

Art, Vendors and Forgery

the one that was displayed was a fake. But I'm not so sure the real Rodriguez is lost."

She didn't protest. She didn't shout. So I went on.

"That copy you have—the lithograph you claim has the wrong sky—it's breathtaking."

I reached into the room and flipped on the light. She turned her head, and when her eyes landed on the painting at the far wall, her hand flew to her chest. She didn't speak, just stared.

"I think you knew it was the real painting all along," I said softly. "What I don't understand is why you kept it hidden. You love Rodriguez's work. You've said yourself that more people should learn about it. So... why keep this one a secret?"

Mrs. Roberts brushed past me into the room, walking all the way to the canvas. When she turned around, her eyes shimmered with nostalgia—and I suddenly understood.

"You told me you met him," I said. "But you didn't say you were in love."

Her fingers trailed along the edge of the frame, a wistful smile forming. "This cliff... it was near my parents' home. That storm was the last time we spoke. That's why the sky looks like this—so vivid, so angry, so heartbroken."

When she looked at me again, her gaze was misty but steady.

"Sebastian was my first love. He came to my hometown chasing his dream of being a painter and took a job with my father to get by. He wasn't meant for business. His talent was... breathtaking. And his spirit—it needed freedom. He told me one day he was leaving. Said he had to go where people understood his art. That meant leaving me, too."

She sat down, motioning to the chair across from her. I took it without a word.

"I moved to Apple Creek thinking I'd feel closer to him here. But then I met Fred. I fell in love with my husband and forgot about Sebastian—until a few days before our wedding, when he showed up at my door."

I leaned in, unable to hide how hooked I was on every word.

"He asked about his present. A promise he'd made. I told him I didn't know what he meant, and he left—furious. I feared he might do something reckless. I wasn't wrong... or so I thought."

Her gaze drifted to the painting again. "I followed him to the museum. I saw him running out with a canvas, and DeVoir was behind

Art, Vendors and Forgery

him, yelling, threatening to call the police. But Sebastian didn't stop. He tossed the painting into his truck and drove away."

She went quiet. Her eyes shut for a long moment.

"When I found him, he was standing by a fire pit. The painting, now half burned, was beside him, and DeVoir collapsed on the ground, crying. I hid. I was scared—these two men, furious with each other, and I didn't know what would happen. But Sebastian just... left. Got back in his truck and drove away."

"I thought DeVoir paid Scott Durst to authenticate the painting," I said.

Catherine shook her head slowly. "No, sweetheart. DeVoir paid Scott to forge it. I've always hated that horrible fake."

I opened my mouth to ask why she never spoke up, but she answered before I could.

"When I got back from my honeymoon, there was a package waiting for me. Inside was the real painting. On the back, he'd written, 'I couldn't destroy our storm.'"

My hand pressed to my heart as the emotion of it hit me.

"I know," she said gently. "I was young. I didn't want Sebastian arrested. So when De-

Voir unveiled the fake... well, the real painting was safe, and Sebastian was gone. I had Fred. I had my life. Why stir things up?"

"But then DeVoir got promoted," I said softly.

She nodded. "I couldn't stand it. That's why I joined the museum's board, and because I knew DeVoir, I also joined the Historical Preservation Society. I was always on his case, and he learned to hate me for it."

"And then Sebastian died."

Tears welled in her eyes. "I never meant to cause so much pain—to Benjamin, to your family, to Dana. Though I must admit, I'm glad she's no longer with that criminal."

I looked at the painting again. Now I understood the sorrow that radiated from it—the rage, too. It wasn't just a work of art. It was a goodbye, painted from heartbreak. A masterpiece meant for one person. I was lucky just to see it.

I stood up and smiled. "I'm really grateful for your help with the rain backup, Catherine. I'd better get everything sorted for the museum."

She stood too, her eyes flicking from me to the painting.

"Like I said," I added gently, "It's a magnificent copy. And it belongs right here, on your wall. Just like the art festival belongs to the R-Parks staff... and only them. Understood?"

She hugged me—tight, trembling—and whispered in my ear, "Thank you."

Epilogue

After the whirlwind that was Friday—finalizing everything for the festival with what felt like a million last-minute, unexpected details—and then a wonderful but *very* energetic day enjoying the event with Darcy and my family, I was looking forward to staying home.

My sweet sister had been quite serious about dragging poor Paul to the candlelight dinner—formal suit and everything. Ben and my mom decided to go too. I was happy for her. There was no doubt she looked radiant that night, but Ben seemed *overjoyed*. I couldn't help but wonder if I should start checking the real estate listings in the area. I loved living with my mom, but if Ben really

Art, Vendors and Forgery

moved back... maybe it was time for Darcy and me to have our own place.

"Mom!" Darcy's voice floated up from the basement. "Can Toby and I watch the movie again?"

I rolled my eyes as I rinsed the empty popcorn bowl in the sink. "Didn't we just watch it?"

"Please!" they both shouted at the same time.

How could I say no to that? Besides, I was secretly hoping they'd both fall asleep on the couch soon. "Of course," I called back, delaying my descent into the chaos below. "Need any help?"

"No!" Darcy answered. A second later I heard her running feet, followed by giggles and muffled chatter.

The doorbell rang, and I grabbed my purse to pay for the pizzas. I'd eaten more than enough at the festival—Terry had outdone himself with the bake-off and culinary arts—but Darcy and Toby weren't exactly fans of seafood or curry.

When I opened the door, Bruno barreled inside, nearly knocking me over—just in time for me to be smacked in the face with a bouquet of flowers.

"Dear goodness, Bruno!" Logan said, exasperated. "I can't count on you for a subtle entrance."

From the basement, a wave of laughter and playful shrieks rose up.

"I suppose Bruno found them," I said with a smile.

Just then, the pizza delivery guy showed up. Logan awkwardly fumbled for his wallet, his arm still in a sling. In the end, he shoved the flowers into my hands and balanced the pizza boxes with his good arm.

"You didn't have to bring flowers," I said as I led him into the kitchen. "Or pizza."

He set the boxes on the counter and leaned against it. "This isn't going quite the way I imagined."

I narrowed my eyes, still holding the bouquet. "What is this, Logan?"

He cleared his throat and looked at the flowers. "It's an apology, Maggie. A real one. I owe you."

The ridiculous butterflies in my stomach decided now was the perfect time to throw a party, but I kept my expression neutral. "An apology for missing the festival?"

I walked over to the cabinet to grab one of my mom's vases. He didn't know I'd already

Art, Vendors and Forgery

heard the reason he wasn't around. The mayor had let it slip—apparently stepping down as interim chief wasn't as simple as he'd hoped. Logan had gone back to the city to formally resign and be reinstated as a detective, with Bruno officially as his partner. Ben would take over as acting chief again on Monday, at least until Chief Anderson decided to return.

"I'm sorry I missed it," he said. "But I heard it was the best one yet."

"Oh really? Who told you that?"

"I saw your mom and Ben at the candlelight dinner. I was looking for you. They said you were babysitting the little ones."

"My mom's biased, and Ben's probably still grateful we saved his reputation."

Logan chuckled. "Maybe, but it was Mrs. Roberts who wouldn't stop bragging about the incredible job the R-Parks Department did this year."

A swell of pride warmed me, though I couldn't help but suspect her praise came from me kind of blackmailing her during our previous discussion.

"What happened to that painting, Maggie?"

I looked up. He was watching me carefully.

"So *that's* why you brought flowers? Trying to butter me up for information?"

"Nope. But is it working?"

I leaned closer and whispered, "I don't know what you're talking about. The police said they couldn't find it after it was returned to the museum from evidence."

Logan folded his arms. "So that's how we're playing this?"

His tone was more amused than suspicious, so I smiled and took a whiff of the flowers. They really were lovely.

"Thanks for these," I said. "Sorry they were a waste."

"They weren't. And they were for the apology." His expression turned serious. "I'm really sorry, Maggie. It meant a lot that you waited for me in the hospital. But I was... I was mad."

"Mad?" I stood a little straighter.

"Yes! I told you—I don't know what I'd do if something happened to you."

My cheeks burned, and I buried my face in the bouquet, pretending to examine the stems.

"Well, I told *you*—I wouldn't feel any better if something happened to *Bruno*. And I *really* didn't appreciate that you got shot. It was terrifying—and the reason *I* ended up in the hospital. You may not know everything

Art, Vendors and Forgery

about me, but... I'd like to consider you a friend. And that means if something happens to you, I'll be there."

"Maggie," he said, stepping closer, stopping only because of the counter between us, "we *are* friends. We've been friends for years."

"Oh really? How's Dana?"

Logan ran a hand through his hair. "I still don't know how you didn't know she's my ex-wife. But... Dana's doing well, all things considered. She left the museum and is looking for work in the city. I think she's happy to be back in her own house—and out of my mess."

"Your mess?" I asked before I could stop myself. "I didn't think it was *that* bad."

He laughed. "Thanks—I think."

"You want to see a real mess?" I handed him a couple of plates. "Let's bring this pizza downstairs. I'm not even sure we'll find the couch under all the toys and pillows."

He didn't move. "Are we good, Maggie? I really am sorry I didn't—"

I smiled and steadied my trembling hands on the pizza boxes. "It's all right, Logan. I'm glad you're okay. And that Mark is taking time with his daughter."

"Mark?"

"Yes. Mark Warren—your deputy?"

Logan rolled his eyes. "I still don't like him."

I headed down the stairs. "You should be more forgiving. Maybe send him flowers."

Logan pretended to laugh. "You think the kids will share with me?" he asked as he followed. "I haven't eaten."

"No promises," I called back.

As I settled onto the couch, Darcy and Toby snuggled in beside me, the mess of toys forgotten for the moment. Bruno curled up at my feet, and Logan, standing nearby with his pizza, shot me a wry smile.

Maybe we were real friends. Maybe this was the start of something new. And I couldn't help but think that, for once, I might be exactly where I was meant to be.

After all, there was no better mystery than that.

I hope you enjoy this book in the Apple Creek R-Parks Department Mysteries Series and are excited to read the next book; **Cake, Vows and Extortion.**

When something borrowed vanishes...

Art, Vendors and Forgery

**so might the bride.**

Just days before Lucy's dream wedding, a priceless family heirloom goes missing —and her future mother-in-law threatens to call off the ceremony unless it's recovered. With rumors swirling about a nearby diamond heist and suspects hiding among the wedding guests, Maggie Willow is once again pulled into a mystery. But this time, the stakes are high, the timeline is short, and the guest list includes more secrets than RSVPs. With Bruno's nose and Logan's backup, can Maggie uncover the truth before "I do" turns into "never mind"?

If you want to receive updates from future books, behind the scene happenings and short puzzle mysteries, join The Detective's Dispatch group here.

Acknowledgments

For your patience, support, belief in the cause, staying with me and tolerating the time that I took away from all of you to sit down and write. During these years, I learned so much from all of you. For listening to my stories, complaints, and successes. For your help and critiques, for all of these and more,

To Each one of you, who loves to read mysteries and took the time to read my take on them. My amazing coaches; Scarlett and Bryan, my mystery group friends, Mom, Gloria, Teddy, Josephine, and You up there...

Thank you.

About the Author

Hi, I'm Montie Red, and I have a not-so-secret addiction to crafting twists, turns, and mysteries best solved with a cup of tea (or maybe a snack). My *R-Parks Mysteries* series is inspired by my love for quirky small-town charm, meddling sleuths, and the occasional murder that needs unraveling—purely fictional ones, of course!

My biggest motivation is my amazing daughter, who keeps me inspired and grounded. We share our home with two lovable dogs, five chatty birds, and a husband who frequently attempts daring escapes from my writing world—usually by pretending there's a very important game to watch or a mandatory tee time.

When I'm not diving into cozy mysteries, I step through portals to other worlds, writing sci-fi and fantasy adventures under the pen name Monica Red. Whether it's catching a killer or navigating interstellar chaos, I'm always in the thick of an exciting tale.

Thanks for joining me on this storytelling journey. Grab a cozy blanket, dive into a book, and let's solve some mysteries together!

Made in United States
North Haven, CT
20 July 2025

70852778R00152